Waiting
for
Saturday

Catherine Morrison

For Luke & Sophie,
who now think writing is
Mummy's real job.

Chapter One

She heard a scream. Was it her daughter? Was it even a girl? Sometimes it was hard to tell; some boys could be just as high-pitched. Abigail Preston looked over her Kindle to the drama that was unfolding at the foot of the slide. It was just a clash of heads – one of the more common occurrences at the soft play centre. By the looks of it, neither child was hurt, and they were both soon happily back at play. No harm done. She searched the play frame for her daughter and relaxed when she saw her.

She watched for a while, then slipped into a daydream ... until she was disturbed by the buzz of her mobile phone. That innocent little sound always stopped her heart. Praying that it was her sister or best friend, she reached for it immediately. Her whole body tensed when she saw it was her husband Kevin texting. Mentally, she ticked off her list of chores. She was sure she'd completed them all before leaving the house. *There's no way I could have forgotten one. Is there?* She took a deep breath and prepared to read the text.

Football kit!

She groaned and rubbed her temples. She'd washed, ironed and packed his football kit, with his spotlessly clean football boots, in his kit bag, and placed it by the front door. Like she always did. But sending him a text like that would be like waving a red flag to a bull, so she opted for a softer approach. A safer approach.

It's at the front door, honey. x

She texted back quickly then placed the phone on the table. Wringing her hands, she stared down at it. Would there be another message? She wasn't expecting a thank you, but he might claim there was something else she had forgotten to do. His lists were always changing.

A few minutes passed and there was no text. She put the phone back into her handbag and assumed that would be the last she'd hear from him that day. After his football game, he always went to the pub with his mates. *Mates*. She rolled her eyes. They were more like his fan club. They idolised him – the confident, charismatic salesman who had moved out of London to the small town of Grovewood on the commuter belt. At the pub he always bought the first round then propped up the bar and held court. He told outrageous stories and had a huge arsenal of jokes, most of them sexist. He had them all eating out of his hand. Although they probably wouldn't be so loyal to him if they knew what he said about them behind their backs. 'Village idiots' was his go-to insult. He thought he was superior to them because he had lived and worked in London all his life, and thought the people in his new town lacked drive and ambition. But his peers in London were moving out, buying bigger properties outside the capital where money went further, and it had prompted him to do the same.

Determined to enjoy her quiet Saturday morning, Abi drained her tea and returned to her story. She had reached a good part: the increasing tension suggested the killer was about to strike again. She was ready to swipe the page when she was interrupted again. But this time it was by a sound seldom heard in these venues: a male voice.

"Do you mind if I sit here?" he said.

She looked up at him. He was poised to pull out one of the free chairs at her table. He was gorgeous, with thick short brown hair, brown eyes and a clean-shaven face that was perfect in every way. Dressed neatly in blue jeans and a black jumper, he looked like he'd just walked out of John Lewis. And by the way his clothes clung to his tall, toned-looking body, it was a safe bet that he belonged to a gym.

Confused, she sat up in her chair and had a quick look around the large room. There were plenty of other places for him to sit. She turned back to him and, raising an eyebrow, pointed her perfectly manicured finger towards the half dozen vacant tables behind her.

He cracked a nervous smile as she glared at him. "Oh, I know there's plenty of empty seats. But it's my son's first time here…" He shifted from foot to foot. "I want to sit up close so I can see him."

She thought that seemed fair. After all, she was sitting at the closest table to the play area. "Then you're welcome to sit here," she said politely, and returned to her Kindle.

"Thank you." He pulled out a chair and sat down beside her.

Henry Archer tried to make himself comfortable. He'd never been to a soft play place before. He preferred to take his son Toby swimming, or to the park, but Toby had left his swimming gear at his mum's house and it was far too cold for the park. He looked around the room. The play frame looked safe and entertaining enough for the four-year-old, the café looked well stocked with treats, and he had a very nice view of the woman he was sharing the table with. An unexpected bonus.

He watched Toby play, but after a few minutes he sneaked another glance at the woman out of the corner of his eye. He thought she was beautiful. She had straight, shoulder-length blonde hair, incredible blue eyes and perfect sun-kissed skin – at the end of January, this suggested that maybe she'd been lucky enough to have had a winter holiday. He couldn't see much under the table, but she was definitely slim. The conservative neckline of her expensive-looking blouse hinted that it concealed ample breasts, which he wouldn't mind seeing up close. Then he noticed her left hand. By the size of her solitaire engagement ring and diamond-encrusted wedding band, he knew she was more than likely the owner of the brand-new Audi Q7 SUV he'd seen in the car park. He sighed and turned his attention back to the play frame.

But his gaze eventually returned to her. He was unable to stop himself. She was so immersed in her book that she didn't even notice him looking. The hint of a smile on her face indicated she was enjoying the story. He assumed it was a slushy romance and, since he enjoyed reading those too, among other things, he was confident he could use her book as a conversation starter. He tilted his head in an effort to catch her eye. "I'm Henry, by the way."

She shifted her glance from the Kindle just long enough to give him a half smile.

"Do you come here often?" he continued.

She let out a long sigh.

He couldn't blame her. That was such a cliché. He cleared his throat. "I'm sorry. I wasn't trying to hit on you. I'm just not sure of the etiquette. I've never been to one of these places before."

She gave another sigh, but this time accompanied it with an eye roll.

Henry could feel his cheeks beginning to burn and he wanted the ground to swallow him up. "I'm sorry. I can see I'm disturbing you. I'll leave you in peace to read your book." He turned back to the play frame.

It was obvious that he was frazzled, and Abi was sorry to have added to his unease. She thought he was just being friendly, but this was *her* time. The only time in the week that she had a few minutes to herself and wasn't busy with school runs, after-school activities, housework and her ever expanding list of errands. All she wanted to do was relax and read a book, not make chit-chat with a complete stranger. But he did seem nice, and he looked like he needed help. She placed her Kindle on the table and tried to make amends.

"I'm sorry, Henry." She made a point of catching his eye. "I didn't mean to be rude. It's just that I was getting to a really good part in my book. I know how you feel. I was lucky the first time I came to soft play, because I had my best friend Glenda to show me the ropes. These places can be intimating for newbies."

Looking grateful, he nodded.

"So, I suppose the appropriate thing for me to do is to pass on the favour. I'll give you a few tips for surviving soft play."

He gave an exaggerated sigh of relief. "Thank you so much! I didn't catch your name?"

"It's Abigail. But everyone calls me Abi. My

husband calls me Abs." She flinched as she omitted his favourite prefix, 'fat'. She adjusted her blouse and forced a smile.

He held his hand out to her. "I'm very pleased to meet you, Abigail."

She felt a little shiver down her spine as she shook his hand. No one ever made the effort to call her by her full name, and she really liked the way it sounded when he said it. His voice was confident, but calm. Suddenly conscious of how her own voice sounded, she cleared her throat before she spoke. "OK, Henry. It's pretty simple. Just let the children play. If someone engages you in conversation, this is what you do."

He put his elbow on the table and rested his chin on the palm of his hand.

"Start by asking the name and age of their child, or children, and comment on their cuteness. You can be as specific or as vague as you like, as long as you're complimentary, and then they'll return the question and the compliment."

He nodded. "Got it."

"Then they will tell a story about their child which is hilarious to them and mildly amusing to you. You can reciprocate, and this step can be repeated as many times as necessary. Once the anecdotes have dried up, other topics of conversation can include, but are not limited to, how your child is getting on at nursery or school, recipes, craft ideas, holidays and the latest TV series. If you're lucky, something juicy like *Strictly* or *The Jungle* will be on and you'll have loads to speak about."

Abi was interrupted by another scream from the play frame. They both looked over to check it wasn't their child in peril, then focused back on each other.

"And try not to get too involved in disputes

between children. Try to let them figure it out for themselves." She held up her index finger as a warning, "But be on your guard for bullying or foul play. It rarely happens, but it happens."

"Thank you, Abigail." He gave her a warm smile. "You certainly seem to know what you're talking about."

His smile was so infectious that she couldn't help smiling back. "One last thing..." She leaned in a little closer to him. "If you don't fancy being sociable you might want to bring a book, or if books aren't your thing perhaps a newspaper or magazine." She held up her Kindle and gave him a stern look. "People *usually* leave you alone if they see you're reading."

"I'm so sorry." He flushed. "Please let me buy you a cup of tea or coffee as an apology and a thank you for your advice."

She pointed to her empty cup and half-eaten scone. "No, thank you. I've just had one. And you're welcome." She reached for her Kindle.

"So, it seems you really enjoy reading. I love books too."

He had her full attention. "Really. What genre?"

"All of them. I'm a bit of a bookworm, it comes with the job. I teach English literature at the grammar school."

She screwed up her face. "I did English Lit for A level. I *hated* it. I'm more a read-for-pleasure kind of girl and some of those books were pure torture." Although if she had had a teacher who looked more like Henry and less like Roy Cropper from *Coronation Street*, she might have enjoyed classes a bit more...

"Yeah, I know some of the classics can be hard going, but more often than not they're worth persevering." He leaned towards her and whispered, "Don't tell my students but I have a guilty pleasure. I love contemporary thrillers."

"Me too." She reached for her Kindle and touched the screen a few times. She held it up to show him the cover of the book she was reading.

"No way! I loved that book. You said you were getting to a really good part... Would the plane be about to land?"

Her eyes widened. "How did you know?"

"That was my favourite part."

They were busy discussing the irony of the main character's fear of flying when a small boy came running towards their table, sobbing. Henry pulled the child onto his knee and tried to console him. "What happened, buddy?"

"Daddy..." – he pointed to the play frame and to a girl who looked like butter wouldn't melt in her mouth – "that girl hit me."

Abi saw the girl he was pointing at and let out a long sigh. She stood up and gave Henry a guilty look. "I'm so sorry. That's my daughter. *Emma! Come here now!*"

The little girl arrived at her mother's side, looking sheepish. She was the complete image of Abi but she had long brown hair, which was tied in pigtails.

"Emma. Did you hit this boy?"

Emma pointed at Henry's son. "He said my pigtails were stupid."

Gasping in horror, Abi placed her hand on her chest. "How could he say such a thing?" She winked at Henry and turned to the crying boy. "I'm sorry. I hope you're all right." She turned back to Emma. "Say sorry!"

8

"No." Emma stuck out her bottom lip.

"OK. Then let's go home." Even though she'd said it with complete authority, it was an empty threat. It was far too early to go home; Kevin wouldn't have left for football yet. Nevertheless, she held Emma's eye until she relented.

"Sorry, *little boy*," Emma muttered.

Abi tried not to smile. Emma wasn't wrong. She was at least a centimetre taller than him. Abi turned back to Henry's son. "Now, cutie. I think you should know that girls take their hair very seriously, so Emma was right to be upset with you. But she should have just talked to you – she definitely *should not* have hit you." She glared at Emma, who was waiting impatiently.

"Can I go back and play, Mummy?"

"Yes, but you're not off the hook. You're going to tidy your room as soon as we get home. And no more hitting, or there will be further, more serious, consequences. Now off you go." She turned back to Henry. "I'm so sorry. I'm trying to teach her to stand up for herself, but she went too far. It's such a fine line."

Henry gave a sympathetic nod. "I know how you feel. But don't worry, it's all right. The hitting aside, that was a valuable life lesson for Toby."

They tried their hardest not to laugh as poor Toby snuggled into his father's arms and dried his tears. After a few minutes, when Toby had composed himself, he went back to play with Emma.

While their children played together, Abi and Henry talked about books – both contemporary and classic. They compared their favourite authors and debated the merits of first-person versus third-person point of view in storytelling until it was time for Abi to leave. She was sorry to go; she couldn't remember the last time she'd talked to someone about books. Her friends were more interested in watching *Game of Thrones*. But she had a long list of errands and housework to do, so she couldn't stay.

Henry stood up and helped her with her coat. One of the other teachers at work had got the same one from her husband for Christmas. He knew from the 'oohs' and 'ahs' in the staffroom that it must be something special. As he slid it onto her shoulders, the smell of lilac caught his nose. He wasn't sure if it was her hair or her perfume, but either way she smelt great. And looked great. She was great, and he didn't want to let her walk out of there and risk never seeing her again. He had to do something.

"Thank you for today. I enjoyed our chat. Do you think you'll be here next week?"

"Yes. I prefer the park, but it's been a long winter and it's far too cold. So we've been coming here every Saturday." She looked down at her feet. "Some Sundays too."

She was there every Saturday? Henry nodded. "I'll probably be doing that myself. I'm newly divorced – well, it's not official yet, but we've been separated for months. I'm renting a flat in that new development on the edge of town. Toby's mum has just joined a Pilates class so I'll have Toby every Saturday morning for this term at least. How would you feel about a standing date?"

She recoiled and narrowed her eyes at him. "I don't think my husband would be too happy about me dating another man."

Kevin wouldn't be happy about her even talking to another man, especially one who was single. Suddenly she panicked. She had been so immersed in her conversation with Henry, she had forgotten herself. She glanced around the play centre, praying that no one she knew had seen them talking. If they had, what would they think? What if word got back to Kevin? Kevin! She realised she hadn't checked her mobile in a while. What if he'd texted or tried to call? He got angry and suspicious if she didn't text back straight away or answer before the third ring. She grabbed her mobile from her handbag. Thankfully there were no new notifications.

Henry threw his hands up in the air. "I'm so sorry. I didn't mean to imply anything untoward. All I meant was that we could keep each other company and talk books while the kids play."

A nervous laugh escaped her. "Oh." That didn't sound untoward at all. Henry was great company. She couldn't remember the last time she'd had a conversation with Kevin about books — or about anything, actually. The fact that Henry was attractive was neither here nor there; there wasn't the slightest possibility that he would be interested in her anyway. He could probably get any woman he wanted, and she wasn't as young and pretty as she used to be. Kevin made that completely clear. And there was no way Kevin would ever find out about her talking to Henry because he'd never be caught dead at soft play — that was women's work. So, there was nothing to worry about — and there was no reason for anyone to be suspicious. Two parents chatting while their children played was nothing to be suspicious about.

Abi smiled. "I suppose I'll see you next week, then."

"I'm looking forward to it already," Henry said

with a grin.

"Goodbye, Henry," she said politely. She picked up her handbag, took Emma's hand and walked towards the door.

As he watched her go, he checked out her backside. He thought she was stunning. Shame she was married. He'd have liked to get to know her better. But he resolved never to think of her like that again. She was also smart and funny. He would enjoy Saturday mornings at soft play a lot more than he thought he would.

Chapter Two

The next Saturday morning at the soft play centre, Abi was sitting at the same table as the week before. She was pretending to be engrossed in her Kindle but was secretly watching the door, waiting for Henry to arrive. They hadn't set a time, but she hoped he wouldn't be too much longer. She had spent the week daydreaming about him and his beautiful brown eyes, and she'd even stayed up late the night before to finish the book. She couldn't wait to talk it over with him and ask if he had read the sequel and whether he thought it was as good as the first.

She had already eaten half of her scone and had topped up her tea with boiling water when the door opened for what felt like the hundredth time. It was them! Suddenly nervous, she held the Kindle close to her face and pretended not to notice as Henry and Toby walked into the play centre.

Toby spotted Emma immediately and ran to join her as she navigated the obstacle course. Henry was inexplicably nervous. He had spent most of the week thinking about Abigail and thought he had exaggerated her in his mind. But when he saw her at the table, engrossed in her Kindle, she looked even more beautiful than he remembered. Her make-up was perfect and there wasn't a hair out of place. Although he was confident she would look beautiful even on a wet, windy day with streaked make-up and her hair in disarray. The blouse she was wearing was very similar to the one she had worn the week before. It had the same conservative neckline, and he wondered why. Abi was probably just a year or two younger than him – thirty or thirty-one, perhaps – but her tops, although flattering, looked as though they had been designed for a much older woman.

He approached her. "Good morning, Abigail. It's nice to see you again." He placed a paperback on the table. "I brought a book this time, in case you don't fancy chatting." Although he really hoped he wouldn't need it.

She looked at the title then nodded in approval. She was over the moon to see him. The last thing she wanted to do was read, so she closed the Kindle and set it down on the table.

"I'd offer to buy you a coffee," he said, pointing to her cup, "but I see you already have one."

"I do. Thank you. I wasn't sure what time you'd be here, so I went ahead. I hope you don't mind."

"That's fine. We didn't arrange a specific time. But we should for next week."

She nodded. "Oh, and for future reference, I don't like coffee. This is tea."

He screwed up his face. "Ew! Black tea? I like lots of milk in mine. Excuse me, I'll be right back." He hurried off to the counter.

She fidgeted with the collar of her designer blouse. She used to like milky tea too but had trained herself to drink it black – milk had far too many calories. She watched him while he waited for his order. He was wearing dark grey combats and a navy hoodie, but he could have been wearing rags and he would still have looked hot. Her mobile phone beeping from her bag made her jump. It wasn't usually so loud, but she had set the volume to maximum in case she got too engrossed in talking to Henry and missed a call or text from Kevin. And the message was from Kevin. It seemed like it was always from Kevin. This time he was reminding her to collect his dry cleaning on her way home. She texted him back, assuring him that she wouldn't forget. She never did. Certain there would be no follow-up text, she put her phone back into her bag and looked back at Henry. After she had scanned him up and down, she focused on his backside – until it suddenly wasn't his backside she was staring at. He had turned and was making his way back to the table. Hurriedly, she focused on the play frame. She hoped he hadn't caught her looking.

They spent at least thirty minutes dissecting Abi's book. Henry had read the sequel and assured her that it was just as good, if not better. The conversation flowed naturally, only interrupted by the children returning to the table for the toast and juice Henry had bought for them. Toby observed that he would rather read Abi's book than his father's, as hers only seemed to have one page. This sparked a whole new discussion about teaching children how to read.

"Isn't phonics great?" Henry asked.

Abi looked down at the table. She didn't think so. She was struggling to get her head around it. Unlike Kevin. The other week he had arrived home early, as he did from time to time, to check up on her. Emma was at the kitchen table finishing her homework when he came in and wrapped his arms around her. "How are you getting on, princess?"

"Just finished, Daddy. Mummy says she's going to check it when she's finished peeling the potatoes."

He tutted. "She hasn't peeled the potatoes yet? What the hell has she been doing all day? I'm starving."

He shot an accusing look at Abi.

Pointing out that he was home early wasn't worth the argument it would inevitably cause, so Abi lowered her head and kept peeling.

"That's OK, princess. Daddy will check your homework tonight. Remember the time Mummy checked it wrong and you got a red mark? We don't want that to happen again. Do we?"

Emma shook her head.

Abi rolled her eyes and placed the pot of potatoes on the hob to boil. *That was months ago.*

"It's OK, princess. Mummy tries her best. Don't you, Abs?" He looked over at Abi, who was about to dunk a plain biscuit into a cup of tea. "Just like that diet she's always trying."

Abi let the biscuit fall into the tea and pushed the cup to one side.

Kevin smiled and turned back to Emma. "Mummy wasn't very good at school – that's why she's just a housewife. But you, my princess, you can be anything you want to be. At least Daddy will be able to be proud of one of his women."

Abi fought to hold back her tears. No matter how hard she tried, she always failed to make him happy. But she couldn't let him see her cry. He'd say she had PMS and tell her not to be so sensitive or, even worse, he'd call her stupid and ask why she couldn't recognise a joke when she heard one.

Abi didn't want to sound stupid in front of Henry, so she tried to sound confident. "Phonics is absurd. It wasn't the way I was taught to read. Or you, for that matter."

"I'm sorry, Abigail. But I think it's inspired."

"You have to say that because you're a teacher.

There's probably some sort of clause in your contract."

Henry recognised the look on her face. He was used to seeing it on his students' faces when they were trying to come up with the answer to a difficult question, hoping that he would move on to the next person. "There's no clause. I think it makes perfect sense. It's OK, though. Your opinion is valid. I think we can agree to disagree on this."

"Phew." Abi pretended to mop her brow, but she was secretly taken aback that Henry had let it go. Kevin would have persevered until she backed down and agreed with him. Then he would have demanded an apology for starting an argument.

"Pst!" He looked around to make sure no one was watching then gestured for Abi to come closer to him. "I didn't get it at first either. But my sister is a primary school teacher. She gave me a book on understanding phonics that she recommends to her parents. I'll bring it for you next week. I'm sure you'll get the hang of it in no time."

He winked at her. The little hairs on her arms spiked; he had a way of making her feel good about herself. "Thank you, Henry. That's very kind." She took a sip of her tea. "So, two teachers in the family? Let me guess, your parents are teachers too."

"No. They're not. My dad's a mechanic, and his dad before him. He inherited the family business and my mum runs the office side of things. My two older brothers work there too. My dad was a little annoyed I didn't join the family business, but I'd always wanted to be a teacher. Then my sister, who's just a year younger than me, followed me into teaching. But she didn't get the same grief as me because I'd already broken the mould. Then to top it off, she ended up marrying a guy who works for my dad, so apparently that counts as keeping it in the family. How about you? Do you have any siblings?"

"Just one. Evelyn. She's four years older than me. She lives in Milton Keynes with her husband and three children. We're very close – Emma adores her cousins. We go up there nearly every Sunday for lunch."

"Every Sunday? That's a lot of driving."

It's better than being at home. Abi forced a smile. "My brother-in-law's parents are from Mumbai. He was born and raised here. Every other Sunday, he cooks amazing traditional Indian cuisine. That's worth the drive alone."

"What happens on the other Sundays?"

"Evie does a roast dinner. That's nice too, but…" She grimaced and shook her head.

They were swapping amusing stories from their childhoods when they were interrupted by a woman calling from across the room.

"Abi!"

Abi looked up to see Janet approaching their table. Her youngest daughter was in Emma's class. Janet was in her late thirties, and very pretty. She was divorced and had a bit of a reputation for flirting with the dads at drop-off and pick-up. Shameless, she stared doe-eyed, at Henry. "Abi. Please introduce me to your friend," she cooed.

Abi had been so immersed in their conversation that she had briefly forgotten she was in a public place. She sat up straight and tucked her hair behind her ear. She hoped Janet wouldn't join them. She only had a few more minutes left with Henry and she wanted him to herself. Her cheeks started to burn. *I hope it isn't obvious. What would people say if they knew he was divorced? I can't be seen monopolising the newly single hottie in case people suspect we're fooling around. What if word gets back to Kevin somehow? Henry hasn't mentioned that he's dating anyone...*

She knew full well that he and Janet wouldn't get on, but she decided to let him figure that out for himself. It was a little devious, but really, she was doing nothing wrong.

"Henry, this is Janet. She's divorced, like you."

It seemed that was the only information Janet needed. Her eyes lit up and she offered her hand to Henry.

"Pleased to meet you, Janet." He smiled as he shook her hand, wondering why Abi had said that. Was she trying to fix them up? He glanced over at Abi. The look on her face told him that she wanted him to play along. But he didn't get the opportunity, as Janet made the first move.

"Perhaps we could get a drink sometime. Or dinner? Abi, do you mind?" She reached over and picked up the napkin from under Abi's plate. She took her lipstick from her bag and used it to write her mobile number on the napkin, then handed it to Henry. "Call me."

Abi rolled her eyes.

Henry accepted the napkin, even though he hadn't even begun to think about dating. Until he'd met Abi, dating hadn't even crossed his mind. He would love to date Abi. She was beautiful, had a great personality, and they had so much in common. But she was off-limits. Now he had secured a date with a pretty woman – and she had done all the hard work. Surely it wouldn't be that bad. "I'd love to. I'll give you a call during the week."

"Looking forward to it. Bye!" Janet strutted off, wiggling her bum.

Henry looked over at Abi, who had a little smile on her face. His instinct to play along had been right, and he was thrilled by the fact that they had an unspoken mutual understanding. He knew that they could only ever be friends, but there was no law to say you couldn't secretly fancy your friend. "Thanks, Abigail. You've got the makings of a great wingman ... person."

"I'm glad I could help. But be on your guard, she's already been married. *Twice*."

He gave a little laugh and pointed to the second half of her scone. "Do you ever eat the whole thing?"

I shouldn't have eaten the first half. She adjusted her blouse. "No. And it's a shame to waste it." She pushed the plate towards him.

Chapter Three

Henry was the first to arrive at the play centre the next Saturday. He made himself comfortable at *their* table but thought he'd best wait until Abi arrived before he ordered tea. He had spent the whole week thinking about her and couldn't wait to see her. But he couldn't believe his bad luck. Why did she have to be married? He tried to tell himself that there was no point in getting hung up on her. That's why, despite his better judgement, he had called Janet. He was so busy cringing at the memory of their date the night before that he didn't notice Abi and Emma arrive.

"Hiya," Emma said. She dumped her coat and ran off to find Toby.

Henry looked up to see Abi carefully draping her coat over the back of her chair. "Good morning, Abigail," he said cheerfully.

Abi's heart skipped a beat. She just loved the way he said her name. And his smile, it was always sincere. Unlike Kevin, who always maintained a steely glare, Henry's eyes were smiling too.

"Before I forget..." Henry slid the phonics book across the table to her. "Sorry — I've underlined a few passages and made some notes. Feel free to ignore them and do the same. No need to return it." He paused. He'd written something else on the inside of the cover. It had seemed like a good idea at the time but deep down he knew it was stupid and there was a danger she would take it the wrong way. "Oh, and I put my mobile number inside. Just in case you weren't sure of anything and you wanted to give me a call." He held his breath as Abi opened the book and looked at the front page.

There it was. She ran her finger over his phone number. Theoretically, she wouldn't have to wait for Saturday to speak to him – she could ring him at any time. Having this personal information gave her a little flutter inside. Even though this was only the third time they had seen each other, she felt a real connection with him. She wasn't quite sure what it was, and she didn't care; she was too busy enjoying his company. Then she wondered if he would expect her to give him her number in return. She daren't. Kevin rarely gave her privacy if she took a call in his presence. He always seemed too interested in who she was talking to and why they were ringing her. The one time she'd questioned him on it, he'd shrugged it off. He said he loved her so much that he was interested in everything she did. Then he got suspicious and asked her what she was trying to hide.

"I don't think that will be necessary. But thank you." She put the phonics book into her handbag and checked her phone at the same time. No new notifications. She set her bag down and focused back on Henry. It was time for a change of subject. "So, did you give Janet a call?"

He let out a long breath. "I did. We went out last night. She was *rather* insistent."

Abi rubbed her hands. "Wait! Let me get the tea and you can tell me all about it." She reached for her purse.

"Abigail, please let me." He pushed his seat back to get up.

"Sit." She gave him a stern look. "You paid last

week. It's my turn."

"OK. That's a great idea." He relaxed in his seat and checked out her bum as she approached the counter. Why did she have to be married?

Henry gave Abi a quick review of his date with Janet. He had taken her out for dinner, which had been nice, but the steak was better than the conversation. Not that he was able to get a word in edgeways. He'd spent most of the night listening to her complain about her ex-husbands. There wouldn't be a second date. Not with Janet anyway. He looked around the room. "So, who should I try next?"

"It's not a tasting menu!" Abi scolded him.

He gave her a stern look. "I hope you don't have double standards, Abigail? I've heard the way that you women talk about men like we're pieces of meat."

He was right. Every woman in the place was looking at him with hungry eyes, as if they all wanted to take a bite out of him. Abi didn't want just one bite; she wanted to devour him. But she was married. She couldn't think of him like that. She told herself that it was perfectly possible for a man and a woman to be friends.

She shrugged it off and looked around the room. "Listen up." She pointed at the women in turn. "Married, married, divorced, cohabiting, divorced."

He pointed to a pretty woman in the corner. "What about her?"

Abi giggled. "You're not her type."

"Not her type?" He sat up straight and puffed out his chest.

She narrowed her eyes at him.

"Oh … right! That's OK, there are plenty to keep

me going." He laughed.

She shook her head slowly and pretended to be annoyed at him. But she knew he was only joking. She envied him. She thought back to when she was younger and remembered how much fun she had when she used to date. She'd had a few boyfriends before Kevin but never anyone too serious. Whether it was drinks, dinner or clubbing, she loved the anticipation of something new, but the day she met Kevin she knew she would marry him. He was completely different to all the boys she had dated before – more Harvey Nichols than John Lewis. He was handsome, charming and rich. But he didn't come from money or have a fancy education; he was just really good at his job. He was the top salesman in the company. He was head-hunted so often that he changed job every couple of years, each with a higher salary and an even higher commission. He told her she was the only reason he'd bought the house in town, and he couldn't believe how lucky he was to have snapped up its prettiest girl. That, along with his promises to protect her and provide for her, was exactly what she wanted to hear. Her father had died when she was ten, leaving her and her sister without a strong male role model. Kevin spoiled and flattered her, swept her off her feet, and they married quickly. She thought she had it all. She had been so happy.

Abi was listening intently to Henry telling her a story about an altercation between two teachers that had happened in the staffroom the day before. Completely captivated by the calming sound of his voice, she didn't even notice someone approaching their table. It was Maggie, the head of the PTA at Emma's school. Abi was eager to join as soon as Emma had started school; she couldn't wait to be involved in school life. And it was better than she could have imagined. All the other parents were so nice; they listened to everything she had to say. They even rearranged parts of the fundraising calendar in line with one of her suggestions. She couldn't remember the last time she'd felt so useful and appreciated. There was only one downside. She'd had to beg Kevin to let her sign up for it. He was reluctant to let her spend any more time out of the house. He'd made her give up her weekly yoga class. And that had been when Kevin started his regular inspections of the house. He would run his finger over surfaces and check the ironing was up to her usual high standard. She couldn't be sure it was him, but there seemed to be a lot more fingerprints on the windows than there used to be. Things came to a head one Thursday night when she asked him to move the washing from the machine to the dryer while she was out. He threw his cutlery down and slammed his hands on the table. "Are you serious? You expect me to go out to work and take care of the house while you're off gallivanting?"

"I'm sorry. I just don't want the towels to sit damp for too long. They lose their fresh smell. I thought you could help me out, just this once."

He tutted. "OK. Just this once." He pointed to Emma's dinner plate, which was on the worktop. "Only because I can see you're not coping. And if I wasn't paying a small fortune every month for your mother's nursing home, I would be able to pay for someone to come and help you around the house. God knows you need it." He rolled his eyes.

She lowered her head. She really should have put the wash on earlier. She hurried over to him with the pot of beef stew and refilled his plate. "Thank you so much for your help. I'm sorry I had to ask."

He sighed and lifted his fork. "I'm sorry too. Believe me."

Maggie nodded politely to Henry and addressed Abi, who had quickly regained her composure. "Mrs Preston, thank you for your help at the fundraiser last week, and please thank your husband again." She rubbed her hands and looked at Henry. "His generous donation to the raffle proved quite a boost to tickets."

Henry gave Abi a look of approval while she smiled and tried her best not to roll her eyes. Kevin, being Kevin, had donated a 55-inch 4K smart TV to the raffle. It was worth nearly £3,000 and raffle tickets only cost £2 or £5 for three. The PTA had made a small fortune. But only Abi knew that Kevin hadn't been thinking about how the school would benefit; he'd done it to show off.

"You're a lucky woman. Your husband is amazing, generous and completely gorge— Oops, there goes my son. Sorry. I have to go. I'll see you at the meeting on Thursday." She nodded at Henry and hurried away, calling behind her, "Don't be late."

Abi called back, "I won't." She never was.

Henry looked down at his last season's jumper and faded jeans. By the look of Abi's clothes, jewellery and fancy car, he knew she had money, but he'd never stopped to wonder where it came from. Now that he thought about it, Abi rarely mentioned her husband or talked about their relationship. He assumed Kevin was rich and she didn't work, but he used this opportunity to confirm his speculation. "I hope you don't mind me asking, but what does your husband do?"

She took a sip of cold tea. "He's in sales – financial services. Works in London."

"La-di-da." He nodded in approval.

She forced a smile. "I know."

"Now that I think of it, I never asked you what you do."

"Oh." She scratched the back of her head. "I … I don't work."

But she didn't tell him the full story. As soon as they'd got married, Kevin insisted that she stop work. He said that he earned more than enough and he would prefer his wife to be a lady of leisure. She said no. She really liked her job as an estate agent and didn't want to give it up. At first, he said he only wanted to take care of her, he wanted to make sure she had the best life possible. But when she still wasn't keen, his tone changed. He called her ungrateful. He said most women would jump at the chance to spend their time lunching and decorating their fabulous new home. What kind of woman would rather work than be looked after by her generous husband? Perhaps she wanted to keep on working so she could meet men, show properties to strangers because she was looking for a bit on the side? When she complained that he was being unreasonable he laughed his comments off as jokes, but after a few weeks of his 'jokes', she finally relented.

At first, she enjoyed the freedom of not having to work, but after a few months, when the house was finished and her friends were always working, she began to get bored. There were only so many manicures and shopping sprees a girl could take. She suggested to Kevin that she should go back to work. He suggested that they should have a baby. Abi had always dreamed of having children, but she had thought that there was no rush, she was still in her twenties and thought they could enjoy married life for a few years first. But he insisted, and it wasn't long before she got pregnant. Then, when it was almost time for Emma to start preschool, Abi wanted to suggest that she went back to work, even just part-time, but she decided not to in case Kevin suggested they had another baby. He'd probably insist on it. Even though Abi was desperate for Emma to have a sibling, she suppressed the urge. Kevin was always pointing out her shortcomings as a mother. She didn't think she was capable of managing two.

"What do you mean, you don't work?" Henry said, a confused look on his face. "You're a homemaker! That's one of the hardest jobs around."

She blushed. "It's not that hard. And I suppose I'm lucky to be doing something I enjoy."

"My wife" – he held up his hand – "sorry, ex-wife, was always complaining she wanted to spend more time at home with Toby. But we both had to work full-time to cover all the bills."

Abi's heart sank. She knew most of the mums from school worked so hard that they missed out on precious time with their children. What was wrong with her that she didn't appreciate what she had? Kevin was right. She really was selfish and ungrateful. She gave Henry a little smile. "I know I'm luckier than most. I get to spend so much time with Emma – I really miss her since she started school. So, while she's gone, I do the errands, housework and prepare the dinner. When I pick her up, we do homework and the rest of the afternoon is our own. Everything's fine so long as I have dinner ready for Kevin coming home from work." Without being aware of what she was doing, she ran her finger over a small scar on her temple. Now she made sure she always had dinner ready for Kevin.

"My ex would say that's a perfect life."

"It is." She grinned and tried to convince herself that it was. During the week it *almost* was. She and Kevin ate dinner together and shared a bottle of wine most nights. She would smile and nod as she listened to him brag about his day. She didn't usually add much, as he wasn't interested in anything she had to say. When she did speak, he nit-picked and undermined her. She quickly learned to stay quiet. But although weeknights were just about tolerable, she dreaded the weekends. That was because, every Friday after work, Kevin and his mates went out drinking, and Kevin was a nasty drunk.

"And what does your husband do on Saturday mornings when you're here with me?" Henry asked.

What is he implying? Abi gave him a scolding look.

He held up his hands in defence. "I'm sorry."

"His job is very pressured; he works extremely hard during the week. I like to give him a little time to himself at the weekends … to unwind."

That was nearly true. She *had* to give him time to himself. She always made sure she was asleep when he got home from the pub on Friday nights – at least, she pretended to be so she could avoid his criticism of her every move. On Saturday mornings his hangovers made him hell to be around, so she usually placed a full English breakfast and a pot of tea on the kitchen table and called him just as she was walking out of the door. By the time she and Emma had been to visit her mother in the nursing home, to soft play, collected his dry cleaning and stopped at Sainsbury's, he'd gone to play football. After football he went to the pub and she didn't see him again until he got into bed beside her – if he came home at all. On Sunday mornings she'd leave him breakfast and tea and take Emma to her swimming lessons and then to her sister's for Sunday lunch. When she returned on Sunday evenings, he was almost bearable again.

She hated weekends.

She looked over at Henry and smiled. Saturday mornings had recently become much more enjoyable.

Chapter Four

For another few weeks, Abi and Henry enjoyed their standing date. They talked about books, films, their kids, school, and kept well away from the elephant in the room that was Abi's marriage. Henry didn't even ask permission any more before he helped himself to the other half of her scone, and they looked so comfortable together that people would have been forgiven for assuming they were a couple. The children were also enjoying each other's company. Both talked incessantly about the other throughout the week and loved their soft play sessions.

But Henry spent the next Saturday alone at the play centre. He had arrived at the usual time and made himself comfortable at their table. He had heard that a favourite author had a new book coming out and was looking forward to telling Abi about it. It was only during Toby's third visit to the table to enquire where Emma was and ask what time she would be arriving, that he realised Abi was fifteen minutes late. If he ever got there first, Abi was usually not too far behind. He really hoped she'd just been held up and that it didn't mean she wasn't coming. If she'd given him her number, he could have texted, just to make sure everything was all right. He looked around to see if there was anyone he knew – Janet or that PTA lady – who would have her number. No one. After half an hour he resigned himself to the fact that she wasn't coming. He went to the counter and ordered a cup of tea and a scone and some milk and a cupcake for Toby. There was a pile of newspapers on the side. He placed one on his tray and brought everything back to the table. After he had poured his tea and buttered his scone, he took one bite then set it back down on the plate. It just didn't taste the same without Abi.

But what Henry didn't know was that Abi *had* been at the play centre that morning; she just hadn't been able to bring herself to get out of the car. That was because, that Saturday, Kevin had got up early.

Abi had been busy making his breakfast when Kevin stumbled into the kitchen, still drunk. His designer pyjamas couldn't belie his bloodshot eyes, matted hair and pale, unshaven face. And nothing could mask the putrid smell of stale smoke and beer. He was a mess. If only his clients had seen him, Abi thought.

"Tea!" He slumped down at the table. His head was thumping. Those last few drinks hadn't been his best idea, but he'd been so close to sealing the deal with that young redhead. He'd been gutted when her friend dragged her away. He glared at Abi, who had rushed over to fill his mug with tea. She hadn't been very attentive the night before when he arrived home at 1.30 a.m., feeling amorous. He woke her up and asked for sex, but she refused and turned her back on him. Too drunk to argue, he rolled over and went to sleep. And now she was busying herself around the kitchen, pretending to be the perfect wife, but she wasn't perfect at all. She was selfish.

He managed a smile at Emma, who was colouring in at the other side of the table. At least *she* still did as she was told. "Princess, would you please go and see if the boy has brought Daddy's newspaper yet?"

Kevin had the *Sun* delivered on a Saturday

morning. He thought it made him cultured to read the paper over breakfast; he had a long way to go. Emma nodded and ran off to the front door.

He watched her go then turned to Abi. "Abs, your fried eggs last weekend weren't runny enough and the bacon was tough as old boot leather. Bring your A game today, please."

She didn't respond but checked the bacon quickly. It was fine.

He raised his voice. "Abs, I'm talking to you. Did you hear me? Don't serve me shit on a plate. Again. OK?"

She turned to him and forced a smile. "Of course. I'm sorry."

"Good girl." He grunted.

She smiled as she flipped the eggs. That was the first nice thing he'd said to her in weeks.

Then Emma arrived back with the newspaper. He took it from her and gave her a huge smile. "Thank you, princess. May I say you look beautiful today?"

She curtseyed. "Thank you, Daddy."

"Unlike your mother, who couldn't look worse if she tried. She's obviously lost her make-up bag. Why don't you go and find it for her?"

"OK, Daddy." Emma ran out of the kitchen, excited at being trusted with such an important task.

"Honestly, Abs. It's bad enough that I have to see you looking like that. Please don't tell me you ever leave the house without make-up? If any of my friends saw you, I wouldn't be able to show my face."

She resisted the urge to ask if he had seen *his* face this morning. Without turning, she replied, "I always look my best when I leave the house. But today you're up early and I'm not ready yet."

"Then would you get a move on? I'm starving." He banged his fists on the table. It made her wince.

"Serving up now."

She placed the feast in front of him: two slices of fried bread, two eggs, two sausages, two rashers of bacon, black pudding, mushrooms, a grilled tomato and baked beans.

He clicked his fingers. "Cutlery?"

Abi hurried to the drawer and took out a knife and fork. She offered them to him and he snatched them, rolling his eyes. She left the kitchen and went upstairs to get ready.

She examined herself in the full-length mirror at the top of the stairs; her dyed blonde hair was sitting perfectly as always. It used to be brown until Kevin decided he didn't fancy mousey brunettes any more. Her skin was flawless, her eyebrows plucked and sculpted, and Mother Nature's most recent gift of three coarse black chin hairs had been waxed out of existence. Her size ten designer blouse was tucked neatly into slim jacquard trousers and her bum definitely looked smaller than the last time she'd checked. But all she could do was lament the fact that she used to be a size eight. Her weight gain was probably why her husband didn't fancy her any more. Her mind turned to Henry. She wondered if he found her attractive. She'd often caught him stealing a look at her when he thought she wasn't looking … but then, she was *always* looking at him. But he was probably wondering how she managed to keep a husband at all.

She applied some make-up – not that she needed it – then headed downstairs into the kitchen, to find Emma back at the table drawing another picture. "It's time to go. Shoes, please."

"OK, Mummy. Enjoy football, Daddy." Emma jumped down from her seat and made her way out of the kitchen, but Kevin beckoned her over. He wrapped his arms around her and peppered her cheeks with kisses.

"I love you soooo much, princess. Have a good time."

Abi watched as the two of them hugged, and tried not to be jealous of her own daughter. She did everything she could think of to make Kevin happy – what was she doing wrong? She kept a spotless house, a slim figure and conservative appearance, she kept her opinions to herself and didn't question him on anything. She did everything he asked, even when that meant sacrificing something she wanted or having sex when she didn't want to… That was it! For the first time in ages, she'd turned him down the night before and now he was giving her the cold shoulder. How long would it last this time?

She was about to follow Emma out of the kitchen when Kevin coughed to get her attention. She looked at him. He was pointing to his cheek. Relieved, she leaned in to give him a kiss. Just as her lips were about to meet his cheek, he recoiled.

"I thought you said you always looked well when you left the house." He shook his head and gestured to his plate. "These eggs are too runny. And I've told you umpteen times that I like my mushrooms halved – these are quartered. Do you need me to write it down for you? I'll bet next-door's dogs are better fed than me. I'm only forcing down this swill because I'm starving. I may or may not come home for dinner tonight, but have something edible ready for me, if you can manage that, Fat Abs." He shooed her out of the kitchen.

Abi skipped the visit to her mother and cried quietly all the way to the soft play centre. *I can't believe I've upset Kevin again. He works so hard and needs a loving, supportive wife, not a train wreck like me. I can't even get the mushrooms right, although I could swear blind he told me he prefers them quartered. If it wasn't for Emma, he would probably have left me by now. I have to do better.*

Abi pulled into the car park of the DIY store opposite the soft play centre and stopped the car. She pulled down the sun visor and looked at herself in the mirror. Her eyes were puffy and her make-up was streaky. She took a few deep breaths in through her nose and out of her mouth, trying to compose herself, but after a few minutes Emma started to get restless.

"Aren't we going in, Mummy?"

At that moment Abi saw Henry's car turn into the soft play car park. She ducked down behind the steering wheel. There was no way she could go in there. He couldn't see her like this. No one could. But she couldn't go home yet. She thought quickly. "I'm sorry, honey. I forgot I told Jenny's mum we'd meet her at the park today. Silly Mummy." She drove out of the car park and towards the motorway in search of a park where she was certain she wouldn't see anyone she knew.

Chapter Five

The Saturday after their missed playdate, Henry was the first to arrive at the play centre. He tensed every time the door opened, then his shoulders slumped when he saw it wasn't Abi. He sipped his tea and desperately hoped she would show up today. Because, if she didn't, it could only mean one of two things. Either she was fed up with their standing date or something bad had happened to her. He needed to find out, and if she didn't show up, he would just have to engineer a meeting. He'd been hanging on her every word for weeks, so he knew which dry cleaner she used, which school Emma went to, and which Sainsbury's she preferred. After soft play, he would drop Toby back to Becca's and then hang out at Sainsbury's until he 'accidentally' bumped into her.

He was trying to decide if his plan was cute or creepy when the door opened again. This time it was them. Emma handed her coat to her mum and headed straight for the play frame. Abi spotted Henry immediately and made her way to the table. The sight of him almost made her heart jump out of her chest. Two weeks had felt like a long time: it had taken all her self-control not to retrieve his mobile number from the phonics book. Once she'd crossed that line, there would be no going back, and it might be the first of many lines.

Henry stood up and held out his hand for their coats, which he draped over a spare chair. As he sat down, he looked her in the eye. "Am I glad to see you! What happened to you last week? I was worried about you."

The fact that he had been worried about her meant he'd been thinking about her. She wondered if he was thinking about her in the same way that she was thinking about him. She tried not to overthink it and changed the subject to something a little less intimate. "Why? Was there a woman you liked the look of and you missed your wing-person?"

"Something like that." He winked. "I'll get your tea."

She watched him approach the counter. The young assistant serving him was giggling and flushed. He had that effect on everyone. Kevin did too but he relished it, manipulated it and expected it. Henry didn't even seem to notice – or to care.

He arrived back with tea and a scone which he immediately cut in half, buttered and spread jam on. He picked up his half before pushing the plate towards Abi. "So, what happened to you last week? Two women hit on me and I really needed your vote."

She took a sip of her tea and didn't answer. "How did you decide which number to take?"

"I didn't. I took both."

But what he didn't tell her was that he had absolutely no intention of calling either number. He only had eyes for Abi. No one else could come close. He thought she was perfect and she was on his mind day and night. He'd even told his best friend Steve everything about her. Well, everything apart from the fact that she was married.

In an effort to conceal her jealousy at the thought of him dating, she punched him playfully on the arm. "Womaniser!" That was the first time she had been brave enough to touch him, and she wanted to touch him again.

He cowered away, pretending to be hurt, but he was more than thrilled by her touch. It gave him the confidence to ask her the question he'd been agonising over in his head. Although he enjoyed their ninety minutes at the play centre each Saturday, he wanted to spend more time with her. "So, Abigail, it's half term next week. I'm off school too and Toby's mum is working, so I'll have Toby every day. Do you want to do something with me? I mean, do you and Emma want to do something with me and Toby?"

Abi thought that sounded like a great idea. Although it was only Emma's second half term, the first one had been quite hard. Emma really missed her friends, and Abi found the days long. It was just a bonus that Abi would enjoy the company too. She hated waiting for Saturday so that she could see Henry.

"That sounds OK. What did you have in mind? If it's nice we could have a picnic at the park and if it's raining, we could try the museum or the cinema."

He shook his head. He'd meant something a little less … public. Abi always seemed a bit on edge at soft play, and they were often interrupted. Things would be more relaxed in a different environment. Just because she was married, that didn't mean they couldn't spend a bit of time alone together. It wasn't like they were having an affair, was it? But agreeing to see each other away from the soft play centre … did that constitute the beginning of an affair? *Could I be her bit on the side? Spend time with her and then watch her go home to another man? Unless … what if she left her husband? No, this is getting out of hand. I wish I hadn't said anything now. But what if that's what she is expecting? Shit, maybe this is something we should talk about when we're alone together. That's what we need – to be alone together.*

"How about a playdate at home? It will be a bit more casual."

It took all her effort not to scream 'yes'. She enjoyed every minute of their time together at the soft play, but she was always on edge in case someone saw them and suspected they were having an affair.

But they weren't having an affair. She'd never consciously contemplated it before. Yes, Henry was lovely, and she was allowed to find him attractive. He was also funny, interesting, and always had something nice or positive to say. She knew from watching him with Toby that he was affectionate, patient and kind. It was sad that she couldn't say those things about Kevin. He was always irritable and got angry at the drop of a hat. But that was mostly because of her – she knew she was a disappointment to him. But what was she thinking? Henry wasn't interested in her. He was obviously just being friendly. There was no reason that she and Emma couldn't meet up with Henry and Toby, because they were friends and that's what friends do. "That sounds OK. We can come to you."

He screwed up his face. "Actually, it would be better if we came to your place. My flat is so small, you can barely swing a cat in the living room. And it's on the first floor so there's no outside space. I'll bet your house is lovely. Where do you live?"

She tried to avoid eye contact. "Richmond Hill."

"Wow! More than lovely. I'll have to get my tux from the dry cleaners."

She used that as an excuse to playfully punch him on the arm again. But this time it was more of a gentle caress while she pictured him in a tux.

Then she panicked. She couldn't have a man come to the house, even with a child. What if a neighbour saw a strange car in the driveway and said something to Kevin? Or what if he came home early? It was too risky. Kevin would hit the roof if he found another man in his house. She was about to tell Henry that it would have to be his place or nothing, when she had an idea. A little smile crossed her face. "I suppose that would be fine. I think the weather forecast said it's meant to be nice on Monday, so I'll put up the bouncy castle."

Henry bit his lip and nodded. "The forecast for Monday looks great."

Chapter Six

Henry took the last left turn off Richmond Road and onto the cul-de-sac which boasted the cluster of seven luxury properties that made up Richmond Hill. These houses were some of the nicest in town and always commanded a high price when they came onto the market. Abi's house was number five. There were three cars on the street outside her house. They didn't look like they belonged in this street either, and actually made his Ford Fiesta look more at home. He assumed that one of her neighbours must be having a party, so he parked a little further down the street. He was already regretting his choice of black cargo shorts and dark green T-shirt. When he stepped onto Abi's driveway, his jaw actually dropped.

Her house was detached with two storeys, a double garage and a beautifully landscaped garden. It was a mansion compared to his two-bedroom flat. Now there was no way that he could ever let Abi see where he lived. Could he even give her the flowers he'd bought for her at the service station at the end of the road? At £10, they'd been the most expensive bunch. He held on to them tightly and tried not to be intimidated. He was proud to be a teacher and it gave him a great deal of job satisfaction. He knew it was the wrong profession to be in if he wanted to make lots of money, but he'd never wanted to do anything else. It certainly wasn't an easy job, but he always maintained that school didn't have to be a chore. He approached lessons with enthusiasm and encouraged laughter and friendly debate in the classroom. The best part was seeing the understanding on his students' faces when something finally clicked, and it filled him with pride to see them succeed. But he wasn't a pushover; he had high expectations for all his students, no matter their ability.

Before he could reach for the bell, Abi opened the front door and greeted them with a huge smile. Henry almost dropped the flowers when he saw her – she looked incredible. Her hair, usually perfectly straight, was tied up in a bun. But a few strands had come loose, giving her a tousled look that he knew usually took ages. She was wearing a stylish white hoodie, tight jeans and crisp, clean tennis shoes. Although her outfit probably cost more than the contents of his entire wardrobe, she looked casual and relaxed in comparison to her more conservative soft play attire. Words escaped him, so he simply offered her the flowers.

"Thank you. But you shouldn't have. Come on in." She reached out and took Toby by the hand. "Emma can't wait to see you, cutie."

Henry followed Abi as she led Toby through the impressive marble-floored hallway and into the kitchen. He was so transfixed on her backside, which looked totally awesome in those jeans, that he didn't hear the voices in the kitchen. When he looked up, he was startled to see three other women and a baby in a highchair sitting around the huge oak dining table.

"Emma, Toby is here!" Abi called into the garden.

Henry looked out to the garden, which was the size of a small football field, to see Emma with five other children. They were climbing on the huge play frame and crashing into one another on the bouncy castle. Emma hurried to the back door and beckoned for Toby to follow her outside. He ran off to Emma.

"Everyone! This is Henry," Abi said proudly to the other women. "And that was his son, Toby. He's in Reception too, but he goes to the other school." She wasn't being facetious. There were two primary schools in Grovewood; there was no difference between them, she was just saying he went to the other one.

"Henry, please make yourself comfortable. Would you like tea or coffee?" She gestured to the state-of-the-art coffee machine, which was big enough to be on loan from the local Starbucks.

The question took him by surprise. He was about to playfully scold Abi because she knew full well that he didn't like coffee, when he realised that she was probably trying to downplay their familiarity with one another. He'd better play along.

"Tea, please. Lots of milk." He took a seat at the table, unnerved by the three sets of eyes that he suspected were mentally undressing him. But the only set of eyes he was interested in weren't even looking in his direction. He watched her at the sink as she filled a crystal vase with water, then followed her to the counter where she arranged the flowers in it. This really wasn't what he'd had in mind. He knew she was married, and he would never act on his feelings for her, but he had thought she felt the same way about him. Of course they couldn't be *romantic* together, but they could still enjoy time *alone* together. Perhaps he had got it wrong and she was just being friendly, but he was there and he was going to make the most of the afternoon with her. Even if they did have eleven chaperones. He put on his best parent-teacher meeting smile and looked around the table. "Good afternoon, ladies." And with those three words he had them all eating out of his hand.

The afternoon went well. Henry remembered Abi's playdate playbook and asked her friends questions about their children and swapped funny stories. Thankfully, he'd overheard a few of the female teachers in the staffroom talking about a show called *Luther,* so he knew the guy they were lusting over was good-looking and not at all like the Gene Hackman portrayal of Lex Luthor he would have otherwise presumed.

He tried not to stare at Abi as she busied about the kitchen, making sure that everyone's cup was topped up and that the children had enough juice and homemade treats. She was the perfect hostess.

"Do you have any other children, Henry?" asked one of the women.

"No. My ex wasn't keen to have another, so it's just Toby. For now."

Abi raised an eyebrow. "For now?"

He sat up straight. "Yeah. I'm only thirty-two. I hope to meet someone else, maybe get married again and hopefully have more kids."

"Kids. Plural?" She laughed.

"Plural. I love kids. I'm from a big family. Both my brothers have three and my younger sister just had her twenty-week scan with her second."

"That's a lot of kids."

"Yeah. Sunday dinner at my parents' house can be quite busy."

After an hour or so of chit-chat, Abi left the kitchen to see one of the women out. Henry used the opportunity to find out a bit more about Abi. He wanted to know everything about her, and who better to ask than her best friend? "So, Glenda, how long have you known Abigail?"

"Since Year Eight. We sat beside each other in history and we've been inseparable ever since."

"That is a long time. Tell me a little about young Abigail."

Glenda smiled and shook her head. "You wouldn't have recognised her back then. She used to be really wild."

"Wild? Abigail?" He was taken aback.

Glenda smirked. "We were always getting into trouble at school. Nothing major, just little things like skipping class, kissing boys in the corridors, smoking in the toilets. But one Friday afternoon we got busted for sneaking a bottle of Lambrini into the common room. Our headmaster said it was the last straw. He put us on permanent detention."

Henry gasped. "As a teacher, I can't condone that sort of behaviour. I have to be on the headmaster's side."

Glenda stuck her tongue out at him. "Well, he didn't follow through. Abi got us out of it by offering to help out with school events and fundraisers – she's really great at planning and organising things. At the weekends we would tell our parents we were going to the cinema and then for ice cream, then we'd get the train into London. On the way there we would plaster ourselves in make-up and drink a bottle of something cheap and barely alcoholic. We would try to get into clubs, but we always ended up in a McDonald's sharing a milkshake before the last train home. That was, until we left school. We weren't interested in university or anything like that – we got jobs in the same supermarket and got a pokey flat together. We worked all week and partied at the weekends, sometimes in town but mostly we went up to London. I was dating

Robbie by then – he's my husband now – and Abi had guys lining up to give her their phone numbers. She was always really popular. We went on like that for about two years, then one Saturday morning Abi and I had to work the early shift. We'd been out late the night before and—"

"Stop right there!" Abi scolded, walking back into the kitchen. She pointed her finger. "Don't you dare tell the rest of that story, Glenda!"

Glenda giggled. "I have to, Abi."

"She has to, Abi," Henry begged.

Abi looked between Henry and Glenda and shrugged her shoulders, trying to conceal her embarrassment. She loved her memories of those days running around with Glenda and Robbie – they were the best of her life. It wouldn't hurt to let Henry know that she hadn't always been so prim and proper. She nodded.

Henry gestured for Glenda to continue.

"We'd been out the night before and we had epic hangovers. Saul, our manager, had a real thing for Abi but she wouldn't go out with him, so he was always kind of a..." – she mouthed a rude word so her baby wouldn't hear – "to her. He saw that she was hungover that day and, as an act of sheer evil, told her to work on the cheese counter."

Everyone at the table braced themselves. Glenda smirked. "Let's just say, the first customer got a whole lot more than the wedge of Cheddar she asked for."

Henry burst out laughing. "She didn't!"

"She did. Not just once. And not just over the Cheddar! She puked over the entire cheese counter and the customer got a nice spray too. Saul fired her on the spot, but not before she puked on him too. To this day,

47

it's the funniest thing I've ever seen."

Henry turned to Abi and gave his best schoolteacher look. "I'm guessing you don't eat cheese any more."

"I love cheese more than ever." Abi began to laugh too.

Everyone was still chuckling as Henry composed himself. He was enjoying hearing about Abi and he wanted to know more. "So, what did you do for a job after that?"

"I got a job in an estate agent. It was answering the phones at first, but after I had been there a few months I asked if I could learn how to show houses. Amara, the manager, said I could shadow Cameron for a while. He was the top earner and liked to show off, so he was thrilled to have an audience and someone to carry his stuff. After a few months, when Amara thought I was good enough, I got to do it full-time. I convinced her to give Glenda my job answering the phones. She was bored at the supermarket and I missed seeing her every day after she'd abandoned me."

"I married Robbie! I had to move out," Glenda pleaded.

"That's no excuse." Abi gave Glenda a loving smile.

Henry watched her looking at Glenda with such affection. Abi was such a kind-hearted person. He really wished that Abi was single, he just knew they would be great together. But the next voice that spoke brought him straight back down to earth.

"Oh, the estate agent – isn't that how you met Kevin?" the other mum asked.

Henry noticed Abi looking at him out of the corner of his eye. He kept his gaze fixed on Glenda, who continued the story, but with what Henry thought was a little less enthusiasm.

"One afternoon I took a call from a businessman from London. He said he was coming to town the next morning and wanted to see our most expensive properties. He wanted as many viewings as we could fit into the morning because he needed to be back in London that afternoon. High-end properties were usually down to Cameron but he was on holiday, so Amara sent the next best thing. The following morning, dressed in her killer little black dress and armed with a handful of property brochures, Abi left the office to meet Kevin Preston."

Abi sighed and began to fidget with her hair.

Glenda continued. "Just before lunch, Kevin called the office. He said he'd take the Richmond Hill house and the 'sales chick' too. I thought he was hilarious and put him through to Amara. He told her he'd pay the full asking price, but only if Abi could have the rest of the day off. He wanted to take her for lunch."

The other woman laughed and fanned her face. Abi and Henry sat quietly as Glenda continued the story. "Guys, it was like a movie. Flowers arrived at the office daily. Kevin whisked her off to spas and fancy hotels and showered her with expensive gifts like jewellery, perfume, clothes and shoes. He was great fun on nights out too – he splashed his cash and always had great stories to tell. Robbie and I loved hanging out with them. After about three months of dating, he surprised Abi with a trip to Paris for the weekend. We weren't overly surprised when they came back engaged. They got married soon after at a country house in Somerset. It was amazing."

"Oh my goodness, Abi!" the other woman said.

"That sounds like a fairy tale."

Abi gave a half smile. "It was," she said quietly, then changed the subject.

Abi began to get nervous as she closed the door behind the second mum to leave. It was nearly half past four and she still had to get everything tidied up, bath Emma and get the dinner on, and Henry and Glenda were still here. Henry had to leave before Glenda did. She couldn't risk being alone with Henry if Kevin came home. He was insanely jealous of her talking to men – any men. She wasn't even permitted to have workmen in the house unless he was there.

She tried hard to regain her composure as she walked back into the kitchen. "Henry, look at the time. You said you had to be away by four, and it's half past."

He gave her a confused look as she parcelled up some homemade scones and cupcakes for him to take home. She offered them to him and gave him a nod. "Remember, your appointment?"

He wasn't sure what was going on but could read Abi's subtle little signals – he knew he had been handed his marching orders. He stood up and called into the back garden. "Toby! We're ready to go." He turned back to Abi. "Thanks, Abigail. I forgot the time."

"That's OK. I'll see you out." She ushered him and Toby out of the kitchen, then hurried past them and had the front door open in a flash.

"Did we outstay our welcome?"

"No, of course not. It's just I need to talk to Glenda privately before she goes … women's health. She's got a little problem and wouldn't feel comfortable talking about it with you here."

"Less said. Thank you for this afternoon – it was

great." He looked down at the floor. "But I wasn't expecting the other mums."

Abi blushed. "I'm sorry. I know it sounds prudish, but I didn't think it would be appropriate for me to have a single man in my house. What would the neighbours think if they saw a strange car outside?"

Henry began to fit the pieces together in his head. She had orchestrated the whole afternoon so they could spend time together. OK, they weren't totally alone, but it was a step up from the soft play centre. He was overwhelmed. Perhaps she did feel the same way as he did.

"So that's why you wanted to come to my place?"

"Yes." Her cheeks grew redder.

"Oh, I'm so sorry. I didn't realise. How about my place tomorrow then?" He winked.

"I can't. I've got a swimming date with Glenda and the kids."

He lowered his head and pretended to sulk.

"How about Wednesday?"

"Wednesday is great. Any time after twelve. And come hungry, I'll make lunch."

"You're going to make lunch for me?" She placed her hand on her chest. "I won't know what to do with myself. I'll feel like a princess being waited on hand and foot."

"Don't get too excited — it won't be anything fancy, just some sandwiches. Doesn't your husband ever cook for you?"

Since they'd been married, Kevin hadn't even made her a cup of tea. "Not usually."

"By the way, you know Toby and I love swimming. Why can't we join you?"

She gasped. "Because I'd be in my bathing suit."

"And I'd be in mine." He puffed out his chest and flexed his shoulder muscles.

Abi giggled. "It's not appropriate. I'm a married woman. We'll see you on Wednesday." She pushed him out of the door. Her pulse was racing as she closed the door behind them and watched through the side window as Henry and Toby skipped down the driveway.

Being alone with him in his flat wouldn't be appropriate either, but she *was* going to do that.

Chapter Seven

On Wednesday afternoon, after a lunch of bacon sandwiches washed down with two pots of tea, Abi and Henry relaxed on the sofa. They were sitting as close to one another as they could without actually touching, watching the children playing snakes and ladders on the floor. Abi loved watching Emma play with Toby. She had never intended her to be an only child and would have loved at least one more. But it had been during her pregnancy with Emma that her life had fallen apart so, as much as it hurt, she suppressed her desire for another child. Luckily, Kevin never brought up the subject of wanting another child. Abi didn't want to put any ideas in his head. She prayed that he would be content with one. Even though he thought she was an inconvenience at times, Emma was his princess. His pride and joy.

She tried to distract herself from her thoughts by looking around at Henry's living room. It was sparsely decorated with a sofa, an armchair, a nest of tables and a media unit. She couldn't help but notice the absence of *something*. She turned to Henry and frowned at him. "No wonder you didn't want me coming here. You were afraid I'd find out you were lying."

He sat up straight. "About what?"

The perplexed look he gave made her laugh.

"The fact that you like books. I don't see any … not a single one."

His eyes lit up and a mischievous grin spread across his face. "That's because they're in my bedroom.

Come on and I'll show you."

She brought her hand to her chest. "I can't go into your bedroom. I'm a married woman – it wouldn't be appropriate."

"Oh behave, Abigail! What do you think I'm going to do? Throw you onto my bed and make mad, passionate love to you?"

He wanted to.

She wanted him to.

"I won't. At least, not while the kids are in the next room." He winked. "I swear the books are in there and you don't even have to go in, you can see them from the door."

"OK then. Let me see."

He took her hand and pulled her up from the sofa. He was amazed that she let him hold on to it as he led her to the bedroom. When they got to the door, she let go of his hand and leaned up against the frame. She looked inside. There wasn't a bookcase, or even a shelf. But there were three huge boxes filled with books. "That's a lot of books." She went into the bedroom and began to root through the nearest box.

The sight of her bending over almost made his knees go weak. If she was to give him even the slightest hint that it was something she wanted, he really would throw her onto the bed and make mad, passionate love to her. He tried to expel the thought from his mind. He knew Abi well enough to know that she wouldn't act on her feelings.

"That's nothing. There are five more boxes in one of the offices at my dad's garage. I'm not sure what I'm going to do with them all."

"How did you end up with so many?"

"They just built up over the years. I bought most,

got some from school and some were gifts. I never throw any away. I'll lend them, but I always ask for them back. Before Becca and I sold the house, we kept them in the second biggest bedroom. She called it the library. I'll get a bigger place one day. I'll get my library back."

Her heart nearly broke. She hoped he would get his library back. She had plenty of space for books at her house and she used to have loads too, but Kevin had made her donate them to her mother's nursing home. He said that reading books was old-fashioned and she should only be reading glossy celebrity magazines so she could keep up with the latest fashion trends – he didn't want a dowdy wife. He didn't know anything about her Kindle, and she was desperate to keep it that way. He loved showing that he was smarter than her, and he wouldn't be impressed that she had been able to find a loophole to allow her to read books, not only defying him but also outsmarting him. It took her a few weeks to save up the money to buy the Kindle because she rarely had access to cash. Kevin insisted she used her credit or debit cards to pay for things. Then he scrutinised her statements. It wasn't because he cared how much she spent; he just liked knowing what she'd spent it on. Once she had the Kindle she couldn't link it to her any of her cards and was only ever able to download free books, or she asked her sister for vouchers as birthday and Christmas gifts.

Becca. Henry rarely mentioned her. Abi had often wondered what had happened between them. From what she could see, there didn't seem to be any animosity between them, and Henry seemed too good to let go. She decided this was as good a time as any to find out.

"Do you mind if I ask why you got divorced?"

He shrugged. "Not at all. Becca and I had only been dating for a few months when we found out she was pregnant. We weren't even living together. We rushed into buying a house and getting married. We thought we were doing the right thing, but it didn't take long for us to realise we'd made a huge mistake. We spent most of our three-year marriage plucking up the courage to end it. We both wanted a fresh start, so we sold the house, split what little was left and we share custody informally. The fairy tale divorce, if there is such a thing."

She hoped her sigh wasn't audible. She was certain that if she ever suggested a divorce, Kevin wouldn't be as accommodating. He was possessive and a formidable opponent in everything he did, and he hated losing. But she tried to shake it off. She didn't need a divorce; they were just going through a bad patch. One that was entirely her fault.

She had another look around the bedroom. A wardrobe, chest of drawers and a bedside table. That was it. No knick-knacks, no pictures, not even paint on the walls. The whole flat needed a woman's touch. "I love what you've done with the place."

"I've only just moved in," he said defensively.

She narrowed her eyes at him.

"OK! It's been six months. I'll get around to decorating sometime. I work all week, I spend Sundays at my parents, and … I've been busy most Saturdays." He stopped and watched for her reaction.

She shifted from foot to foot. She wished away the week waiting for Saturday so she could see him, but she couldn't tell him that. Could she?

"I really enjoy our Saturday mornings," he said

bashfully.

She didn't reply, but the little smile she gave him said more than words ever could. Both positive that they knew what the other was thinking, they stood and looked at each other in silence until Toby appeared at the door.

"Daddy. Can me and Emma have a bist kit?"

Henry looked at Abi for permission. She gave him a confused look.

"A biscuit."

She nodded.

"You know where they are, buddy."

Henry watched Toby run off in excitement, then turned to Abi. "OK. It's Thursday tomorrow so I've only got two days of school holidays left. Abigail, I need your help."

"With what?"

He gestured around the room. "With this bedroom. I saw your house and I know you've got a real flair for decoration, so I want to hire you as my interior designer. Consider those bacon sandwiches you've just eaten a down payment."

Her eyes lit up and she rubbed her hands together in excitement. "You certainly need my help … OK, we'll go to the outlet village tomorrow. They should have everything there that we need."

He nodded.

"I'll meet you there at ten."

He frowned. "We can travel there together. It's not like we're having an affair."

She glared at him. "Why would you say that? That's ridiculous."

"Because you're acting as if we are."

"I'm not acting anything. We're just friends," she

said quickly.

"Yes, and friends *can* be seen in public together."

"We are seen in public, all the time, at the soft play centre."

He shook his head. "Just the soft play, but you don't want me coming to your house and you want to drive separately over an hour out of town so we can go shopping. What's the matter? Doesn't your husband let you have male friends?"

"Of c-course he does." She was lying. He wasn't that thrilled about her having female friends either.

"Then what's the problem?"

"There isn't one. It's just I heard there was a good sale on at the outlet village."

"Oh, OK then. We'll pick you and Emma up at nine."

She panicked. What if a neighbour saw them getting into his car and said something to Kevin? "No, we'll pick you up."

He narrowed his eyes at her.

"My car is bigger than yours. You'll need the extra boot space for all the stuff I'm going to make you buy."

"Go easy, this isn't *Made in Chelsea*. I'm on a modest teacher's salary. Your wedding rings probably cost more than I make in six months."

"Try a year."

"Ouch." He gritted his teeth.

She looked down at her feet. "I never asked him to spend that sort of money. I told him it was obscene."

"Oh God, Abigail. I'm so sorry. I didn't mean to make you feel uncomfortable. If I had his money, I'd spoil you too." He cleared his throat. "I meant, spoil *my* wife."

"I know what you meant." She smiled and

wondered what it would be like to be his wife. But she wasn't. She was just his friend, and she was determined that she was going to enjoy helping him decorate his new flat. "Henry, get a pen and piece of paper. We've got a list to make."

Chapter Eight

The next day at the outlet village they worked their way through Abi's list. The SUV was filling up with paint and painting paraphernalia, new bed linen, curtains and something she told him was a 'throw'. She was delighted when Henry suggested that they go to McDonald's for lunch. A Big Mac was her favourite fast food and she hadn't had one in forever – it seemed that Kevin had a way of sensing when she'd eaten carbs and would crack a 'joke' about her weight. She'd been paranoid for a while and had thought he'd been following her and watching what she ate, then she realised it didn't matter what she ate; she was still fat.

After lunch and a comfort break for the children, they tackled the kitchen supply shop. A spice rack, some tea towels and lots of utensils, some of which Henry thought he'd seen in the delivery room when Toby was born. Henry tried to stop Abi going into the high-end home furnishings shop. He'd been in there before and knew that even the clearance items cost more than he earned in a week. But she insisted that he needed at least 'one nice piece' for his flat.

While she browsed, he tried not to look at anything. The children had been promised ice cream on the way home if they didn't touch a thing.

"Oh, would you look at that?" Abi hurried off to inspect something made of crystal. Henry shook his head. He finally began to look around – not at the items themselves but at their price tags. He definitely wouldn't be making a purchase in this shop. He probably wouldn't even be able to afford a carrier bag. But his eyes were drawn to an exquisite antique-style carriage clock which he picked up and inspected carefully. It was beautiful. Abi arrived at his side and gasped.

"Henry, that would look perfect on your mantelpiece."

He showed her the price tag before he set it down. It was closer to four figures than three. "I couldn't pay *that* for a clock. I can get a nice one in Argos for twenty quid."

She smiled at him then picked up the clock. "My treat."

"No way, Abigail. I can't."

"Of course you can. We're friends, aren't we?"

"Yes."

"And don't friends usually buy other friends housewarming gifts?"

"Yes, but not with their husband's money. To quote you, 'it wouldn't be appropriate'."

She gave him a stern look. "We're married so it's *my* money and I can spend whatever I like."

This was one of the first times she'd been totally honest about Kevin. He didn't care what she spent; her spending money made him look and feel successful. He actually encouraged her to spend, then mock-complained to his friends about her huge credit card bills. He constantly overspent on flowers and gifts for her and Emma, but never discreetly – it was always to prove a point or to show off. Abi had been brought up to respect money and use it wisely, and she rarely spent more than she had to. But every now and then she didn't mind spending his money. Despite what he said about her cooking or the standard of her housekeeping, she knew she'd earned it. But she thought it would be best if she bought herself a little something too, then she'd have something to show for the charge on the credit card. She pointed towards the crystal. "I think I'd like something too."

Henry gasped. "Yikes! What's she doing here? She should be at work."

"What? Who?"

Henry pointed to a woman at the end of the aisle. She was taller and slightly heavier than Abi, with cropped brown hair. She was dressed casually in a T-shirt, boot-cut jeans and trainers.

"Becca. I suppose it would be rude not to say hello. Come on, I'll introduce you."

They walked towards her. She was looking at the same crystal bowl Abi had been admiring. Abi nudged him. "I'd say she had great taste, but she let you go."

He blushed.

"Hey, Becca. What are you doing here?"

Becca took a step backwards. Her eyes darted from side to side and she took a few moments to respond. "Um, nothing. Shopping."

Henry gestured to Abi. "Becca, this is Abigail, Emma's mum and my interior designer."

A smile warmed Becca's face. "It's lovely to meet you, Abi. Nice to put a face to the name. Toby talks about you all the time. And Emma – he's quite taken with her." She looked around until she spotted the children sitting on the floor beside the till, watching an iPad. "That must be Emma. She's beautiful. And those pigtails are to die for."

"Thank you, Becca. And Toby is adorable. A proper little gentleman. Emma says he's the best friend she's ever had."

Henry rolled his eyes. That was Abi's soft play

playbook 101. But he really was surprised to see Becca. "How come you're not at work?"

She shifted from foot to foot. "I just needed a day off. Actually, I should be going—"

Before she could finish her sentence, a man approached. He stopped short when he saw Henry.

Henry did a double take. "Steve. What are you doing here?" He glanced between Becca and Steve, who both looked guilty. Henry's tone changed. "Are you two here ... *together*?"

Abi watched them shuffle nervously, then she turned to Henry and saw the look on his face. He looked devastated.

"I thought you said you'd talk to him," Steve whispered. Not quite quietly enough.

"I told you to do it. You're his best friend," Becca replied.

Henry was now officially in the loop. "How long has this been going on?"

Becca sighed. "Since Thomas's wedding. Remember we were all sat round drinking and you had to go because you had a school field trip in the morning? Steve and I stayed on, and one thing led to another." She looked at Steve, doe-eyed.

"That was months ago, and neither of you thought to tell me? My wife and my best friend?"

Steve coughed. "Eh, soon to be ex-wife ... and I wouldn't say *best* friend."

Henry had gone white. Abi squeezed his arm.

"Thanks, but I'm OK, Abigail. It's just a bit of a shock."

Steve's eyes widened. "You're Abi? I've heard so much about you. In fact, Henry hasn't shut up about you."

Henry shot him a dirty look. Abi and Becca glared

at Steve too. What did he know that they didn't?

Henry felt as if his head was about to explode. Here he was, feeling financially insecure and being bought presents by his wealthy friend who he wished was his girlfriend, in front of his ex-wife and her new boyfriend, who just happened to be his best friend and who knew all about his secret love for Abigail and who had practically just told her so. He wanted the ground to swallow him up. Surely nothing could have made the moment any worse.

There was a loud crash. Then a scream.

"Who owns these children?"

They all looked over to see one of the shop assistants with Emma and Toby. They were all standing next to what looked to be a very expensive, and very broken, Japanese lampshade.

Abi sighed and fished her purse out of her bag. "I'll go."

The others watched as she hurried off towards the commotion.

"That's Abi? She is beautiful. But you didn't tell me she was *married*," Steve scolded. "And to who, Richard Branson? There's more ice on her finger than on the berg that sank the *Titanic*."

Becca shook her head. "An affair, Henry. Really? I'm sure there are plenty of single women out there who would love to date you. And considering the *circumstances*" – she gestured to Steve – "I've got a few friends who would jump at the chance. What about Colette from the surgery? She nearly fell off her chair when I told her we were getting divorced. She said she really fancied you. I don't think she's seeing anyone at the minute – how about I give you her number?"

"No, thank you. I'm not interested in Colette."

"Why not? She's a doctor, she's pretty, funny—"

"Because she's not Abi!" he snapped. "I can't believe I'm even talking to you two about this. But it's not what you think. We're just friends. We've never been alone together. I've never even kissed her on the cheek, for God's sake. And it doesn't matter, anyway. I don't think she'd cheat on her husband even if she had the chance, which she hasn't as we've always got the kids with us. And I don't even know if I want her to cheat. She's so nice and decent, she's got morals and integrity. I don't want her lowering herself like that."

Steve looked at him as if he was insane. "You do know she'd be lowering herself onto you?"

Becca whacked him on the arm.

"Ouch."

"I know. I'm so confused. And you two are together? I'm not sure how I feel about that, by the way." He looked over and saw Abi take the receipt for the broken lampshade from the cashier. "OK. Here she comes, so I'd appreciate it if you two would act cool. You owe me."

They all tried to act cool as Abi approached, holding Emma by one hand and Toby by the other.

"Definitely no ice cream for these two, Henry. And they'd better get good at washing dishes because they have a *huge* debt to work off," Abi said sternly.

Toby suddenly noticed his mum. He yanked his hand from Abi's, ran to his mum and threw his arms around her leg.

Becca kissed Toby on the top of the head. "I've missed you so much, honey. I should have known a week was far too long to let you stay with Daddy." She looked up at Henry, who was looking at Abi, then winked at Steve. "I suppose I could take another day off tomorrow. Steve and I will take you out for the day. How about the zoo?"

"Yay! Can Emma come too?" he begged.

Emma turned to Abi. "Mummy, can I? Pleeeease?"

Abi looked at Henry and then at Becca. They all swapped sympathetic looks. The kids were *so cute*. Becca knelt down to Toby. "It's OK with me, if it's OK with Emma's mummy?" She gave Abi a warm smile.

Abi froze. Her eyes darted to Henry.

"It's all right, Abigail," Henry assured her. "Emma will be in great hands with Becca — she's a responsible parent and a nurse at a GP surgery. And…" He glared at Steve and shook his head. "Well, I suppose Steve is a great guy. I promise you, Emma won't come to any harm. And hey, it would mean we could get a move on with the decorating."

Abi looked around at the five sets of eyes watching her, eagerly awaiting her response. The only time Emma was out of her sight was when she was at school. Kevin didn't like looking after his own child — which he called babysitting — and never let Abi out of the house unless Emma was with her. On the one Thursday a month Abi went to a PTA meeting, when she got home, Emma was still up and hadn't even had her supper. Now Abi was contemplating letting her daughter go off with a complete stranger. But that 'complete stranger' was Toby's mum and Henry was technically still married to her and trusted her implicitly. From what she could make out, Steve was a teacher too, so she guessed he could be trusted. Emma could probably be coerced into not telling Kevin she went to the zoo, so there was just one problem.

Could she be trusted to be alone with Henry?

Chapter Nine

The next morning while Henry fitted Emma's car seat into Steve's car, Abi gave Emma a long hug then had a word with Becca. "Thank you so much for this. And you promise to ring Henry if there are any problems?"

"Of course," Becca reassured her.

Abi reached into her purse and pulled out five crisp £10 notes and offered them to Becca. "For Emma's expenses."

Becca peeled off the top two. "That should cover it. Thanks, Abi. One last thing. Does Emma have a medical condition or any allergies I should know about?"

"Typical nurse." Henry winked at Becca. "See, Abigail, I told you Emma is in excellent hands. Although I don't how good an *art teacher* would be in a crisis."

Steve covertly stuck his middle finger up at him.

"No allergies, no illnesses – just not too many treats, please. Be a good girl, Emma. I'll miss you." She gave Emma a kiss and another long hug before helping her into the car. She made sure her seat straps were tight – probably too tight – then closed the door.

Emma blew her a kiss and waved as the car pulled away. Abi waited until they had gone before she wiped away the tear that had formed in the corner of her eye. She turned to Henry. "She's going to be OK, isn't she?"

"Of course. They'll have a great time." He hoped he would too. He looked Abi up and down. She was wearing what looked like a brand-new light pink T-shirt and black leggings. Was she really going to paint in those clothes? They'd be ruined in no time. Unless she didn't intend to paint... His heart began to race. They were alone together for the first time – perhaps she had something else in mind? He could certainly think of a few things they could do together besides paint. It was best just to double-check. "So, what do you want to do now?"

"Paint, of course. What else would we do?" She hurried off towards the flat. He sighed and followed her.

"You're meant to be rolling right behind me," Abi scolded when she spotted Henry slacking.

But he wasn't slacking. He was very busy staring at her backside and thinking how much he'd love to 'roll behind' her. He tried to focus. She was doing the cutting in and he was meant to be following her with the paint roller. He got back to work – if you could call it work. He was having a great time. Every time Abi stretched up to the ceiling or bent down to the floor, his mind raced. He remembered all the chick flicks he'd been forced to watch over the years. Every time there was a decorating scene, the love interests would end up getting covered in paint and having sex. He really wanted to cover Abi in paint and have sex with her on the dust sheet. He was getting all worked up when he felt his phone buzz in his pocket, which didn't help to defuse matters.

It was a picture message from Becca. He opened it, then let out a loud laugh. "Abigail, you have to see this." He held out the phone to her to show a picture of Emma and Toby in front of an elephant. Becca had staged it in such a way that the elephant looked tiny and the kids looked huge.

"That is so cute. They look like they're having

fun." She was having fun too. Alone with Henry. He looked great in old combats and a tight T-shirt, and the paint flecks in his hair were adorable. But it didn't feel quite right without the children. Abi sighed. "*We* should have taken the kids to the zoo."

Henry nodded. "We totally should have. And Steve and Becca should be here painting my flat. I still can't believe they're together. I knew she'd meet someone someday and of course I'd rather have Steve than some other jackass around my son, but it just doesn't feel right. He's my best friend – I've known him longer than I've known her. He was the best man at our wedding and now he's with her? Allegedly, they've only been dating for a few months, but they seem so close already. I can't help thinking they might have been having an aff—" He stopped himself and hoped Abi hadn't been listening.

But she had been listening. She always hung on his every word. She lowered her cutting-in brush and turned to face him. "Henry, of course it's possible. But maybe it happened like they said; they were just friends and it wasn't until after your marriage ended that they became more. Not everyone has affairs … even though they might really want to." She turned back to the wall and continued to paint.

What was that supposed to mean? Has she really just admitted that she wants to have an affair with me? This is huge. Suddenly his legs felt weak and his head dizzy. He tried to pull himself together. *How does the thought of being with her have such an effect on me? I'm thirty-two, not fifteen. Maybe it's the paint fumes? Maybe it's hunger? That's it – we haven't eaten.* He looked at his phone. Ten to one. "Would you look at that – it's lunchtime. You carry on with the painting and

I'll call you when it's on the table."

She made a smacking noise with her lips. "I'm really looking forward to a bacon sandwich."

"It's not a bacon sandwich."

The sweet smell of pastry caught Abi's nose when she joined Henry in the kitchen. "What's going on in here? Something smells really good."

Henry smiled to himself. This was their first meal alone together and he wanted it to be special, so he'd made a real effort. "It's nothing, just something I threw together. It's the least I could do to thank you for all your help. Plus, as the kids aren't here, I thought we could be a bit more civilised. Please have a seat." He pulled a chair out for her and tucked her into the table. She couldn't remember the last time Kevin did that for her.

The table was laid as if they were at a restaurant: fancy napkins, cutlery, wine glasses and a flower in the middle. He fussed at the worktop then turned to her with one of his new tea towels over his forearm. He presented a bottle of Chablis like a professional sommelier.

She placed her hand over her glass. "I can't. I'm driving."

"Not for hours. You could have one sip, perhaps two." He poured just under half a glass. It was enough for four, maybe six sips, if she rationed herself. He poured the same amount for himself. "I can't be drunk in charge of a paint roller."

Abi laughed. "I don't think I can remember the last time I had wine with lunch."

"Me neither. It's really frowned on in the staffroom."

She laughed again. "Are you this funny at school? I'll bet the kids love you, especially the girls."

"Well, I've had a few batted eyelids, and not exclusively from the girls. But I'm their teacher – *it wouldn't be appropriate*."

She rolled her eyes. "I say that a lot, don't I?"

"At least once every time I see you."

"That's been a lot recently too."

"Yes, and I'm loving every minute of it."

She was too. She couldn't remember the last time she'd felt this way. She loved Kevin but was exhausted trying to please him. Henry was different. He was refreshing to be around, and he never expected anything from her. And he'd gone to so much trouble, organising time alone together, this lunch, the wine. *Wait.* Why was there wine? Was he expecting something from her now? Sex? Was this an affair? It had never felt like an affair before, because the kids were always around. But they weren't there now, it was just them. Alone. Together.

She raised her glass to her lips. Six sips went down in one. "What are we doing here, Henry?"

He was sure he knew exactly what she meant but he didn't quite know how to answer such a direct question. He'd spent weeks trying to play it cool, trying to figure out if she felt the same way about him that he did about her. He didn't dare suggest anything in case it offended her. But this might be the only time they got to spend time alone together. It was as good a time as any to get this out into the open. He took a deep breath and went for it.

"What are we doing in life, in general? Or what are we doing in the kitchen, when we should be in the bedroom tearing off each other's clothes?"

He'd said it. It was out there. He waited for a reaction, but she didn't even blink. Only a few seconds had passed, but he couldn't bear the silence any longer. "Abigail. Do you play cards? Because you've got one hell of a poker face. I haven't got a clue what's going on inside your head."

Her expression didn't change but she took a long, deep breath and looked him straight in the eye. "I'm wondering how soft your lips are. I'm trying to figure out if your touch would be gentle or firm. I'm wondering just how warm your naked body would feel against mine. And I'm imagining how good it would feel to have you inside me."

He grabbed his glass and his six sips went down in one.

"Then I have to remind myself that I'm married."

He jumped up from the table, opened the oven and pulled out a baking tray. "Would you like to taste my quiche?"

"Your what?"

"Quiche. The quiche I made for you."

"You made quiche?"

"Yes. I made quiche from scratch. Would you like some quiche before we get back to painting?" He grabbed the wine bottle and poured himself a full glass. "I hope you don't mind if I have a bit more wine, but I really need it." He placed a bowl of salad on the table and a sliced sourdough loaf. He didn't make eye contact with her. "I wish I was as strong as you."

She didn't feel strong at all, and was trying desperately to hold on to her composure when all she wanted to do was weep. *What the hell is wrong with me? I'm married and I just admitted I want to sleep with another man. I can't do this. I have to put an end to this now.* "I'm not strong." Her voice wobbled. "I have these feelings for you, and I don't know what to do with them. I can't act on them and I can't make them go away." She wiped a tear from her eye. "You've no idea how much I care about you, but nothing can ever happen between us. I'm married and that's not going to change. I don't know if I can trust myself to be around you any more, so I think we should stop seeing each other."

Stop seeing each other? The words hit him like a ton of bricks. He wanted nothing more than to be with Abi, and the thought of never seeing her again made him feel sick to his stomach. There had to be a way he could keep her in his life. He could resist his feelings; he could settle for being her friend. He gave her a solemn smile.

"I'm assuming it's obvious that I have feelings for you too. I know I've crossed the line by suggesting we be more than friends. I've put you in a terrible position. I'm sorry. It was selfish and unfair. I want you to know that I have too much respect for you to put you in a situation like this again. So, I'll be strong enough for the two of us. I won't cross that line again. We can still be friends – all we have to do is try to pretend this conversation didn't happen."

Pretending was something she had become very good at over the last few years. She lifted up her napkin, dabbed her eyes and regained her composure. "What conversation?"

He offered her a plate. "Quiche?"

They ate, quietly at first, but their conversation had cleared the air. Now they both knew where they stood and after a few minutes they were talking as if nothing had happened. Henry didn't even need his extra wine. Abi wolfed down her quiche and asked for seconds. After lunch she refused to let him make any tea, as they still had far too much work to do before the children came home.

Back in the bedroom, they made good progress. Henry did his best to refrain from staring at Abi and channelled his sexual frustration into painting. The second coat was done in no time. They had cleaned up and were admiring the results of their hard work when they heard knocking at the front door. "Our little zoologists are back."

Henry hurried to the door. When he opened it, Toby and Emma burst through into the small hall. Becca was a few seconds behind.

"Well, did you guys have a good time?"

Toby nodded. "Yes, Daddy. I sawed a kangaroom."

"I hope not. It's called a kangaroo and you saw it, not sawed it."

Becca shook her head. "You're both on mid-term – stop teaching."

"It's easier to correct these little things now while he's still impressionable."

"Give him a break, he's just four. Anyway, Steve's down at the car. Do you have Abi's keys so we can switch the seat?"

Abi joined them at the door with her coat and bag. "That's all right. I have to be going now anyway." She threw her arms around Emma. "Did you have a good time, honey? Becca, was Emma a good girl?"

"Yes. She's a credit to you, Abi."

Abi was taken aback. No one had ever said that to her before. True or not, she took the compliment. "Thank you, Becca. And thank you for today – that was very kind of you. I must be going. I hope to see you again." She turned to Henry. "And I'll see *you* at soft play in the morning." She gave his arm a little squeeze.

"See you in the morning. Have a good evening."

"Thanks, I will." And she would. It was Friday, and Kevin didn't come home until late on Fridays. She would have to spend most of the evening reminding Emma not to tell Daddy about her trip to the zoo with Becca and Steve, and she had to come up with an excuse for the £50 cash withdrawal. Kevin was bound to question it. But it had been worth it.

"Toby, I thought you said you needed the toilet. Go!" Becca turned to Henry and raised her eyebrows. "So, did magic happen in the bedroom?"

"If by 'magic' you mean decorating, it did."

"Oh." She grimaced.

"Yes, oh. You'll be pleased to hear that Abigail is still faithful to her husband."

"It's for the best. You don't need to get mixed up in anything like that. Affairs rarely work out."

He squinted at her and wondered why she was suddenly an expert in affairs. Was she was speaking from experience?

"By the way, have you ever met Abi's husband?"

"No."

"Does she talk about him much?"

Henry didn't have to think. For the last few weeks it had become sort of an unspoken rule: they never talked about Kevin. "No. Not much." Then he noticed the look of concern on Becca's face. "Why? What is it?"

"It's probably nothing, but something Emma did today really concerned me."

"What? She's usually such a good girl."

"Oh, she was, but we were having lunch and I'd

ordered a cup of tea. It didn't come with the other drinks and when I reminded the waitress about it, Emma banged her fist on the table and shouted, 'Tea! Now!' I was mortified."

Henry recoiled. "It's not like her to be rude."

"Well, I had to tell her off. But after I did, I asked her why she did it and she said, 'That's how Daddy asks Mummy for tea'."

He dismissed her with a wave of his hand. "She's a kid – they say funny things. Remember Toby told his preschool teacher we tried to cut off his foot when we only wanted to cut his toenails?"

"Remember? How could I forget? For months, I thought every knock at the door was social services. You're probably right. I just thought I'd mention it, in case it sent up a red flag for you. Abi seems nice. I wouldn't like to think her husband is a dick. Anyway, I've got to go. Do you want me to take Toby?"

"No. Do you mind if I keep him? I don't want to be on my own. And we're meeting the girls again in the morning so it saves me coming by to collect him."

"OK, if you're sure. I'll be in all day – bring him back whenever. Bye, Henry. Sorry your day didn't go to plan. Bye, Toby!" she called as she hurried out of the door.

Henry sighed as he closed the door behind her. He wasn't sure if he had a plan. But after what had happened at lunch, he knew he needed a plan. A plan to get over his feelings for Abi.

Chapter Ten

The next morning, Henry was the first to arrive at the soft play centre. He had already had a cup of coffee and wanted another one, but he wanted to wait for Abi. He usually didn't drink coffee, but he was exhausted. He hadn't slept well the night before. Becca *had* sent up a red flag. After she had gone, he started to think about what Emma had said. He recalled a few other things he'd noticed about Abi's behaviour, and was beginning to suspect that there was something not quite right about her situation. Perhaps her home life wasn't as perfect as it seemed. He was deep in thought and jumped when he heard a familiar voice.

"Hey, handsome. I haven't seen you since our date. How come you didn't call?"

He looked up to see Janet, shamelessly posing for his approval. "I'm so sorry. I've been busy with school and stuff. How are you?"

"All the better for seeing you. I suppose you're waiting for Abi?"

Is it that obvious? "Yes, but you're welcome to join us." He'd said the words, but he didn't mean them. He hoped she wouldn't stay.

"No, that's OK. I was just leaving."

"Oh, that's too bad. Er ... have you ever met Abi's husband?"

"Kevin? Yes. He's gorgeous and very charming, but..." She went quiet.

"But what?"

"He can be a bit of a show-off, and..." She trailed

off again.

"And what?"

That was all the persuading she needed. Quickly, Janet pulled out a chair and sat down next to Henry then leaned in close. "I shouldn't really say anything because she's our friend. But my ex plays football with him and says he can be a real asshole. He's ruthless and underhanded – he'll do anything to get one over on anyone. He throws his money around acting the big man, and…" She lowered her voice. "He's always bragging about the women he's sleeping with on the side. Says Abi is far too stupid to notice."

Henry sat back in his chair. "He cheats on her?"

Janet nodded. "That's what I've heard from my ex, but sssh, here she comes." She pointed over his shoulder.

Emma stopped to give Henry a hug before she ran to join Toby. "Hi, Henry."

"Hi, sweetie."

Henry didn't know how to act when Abi approached the table. He needed a minute to process the new information he'd heard. "Good morning, Abigail. It's my turn to get the tea." He hurried off to the counter and Abi joined Janet at the table.

Henry waited for his order and thought about what Janet had just told him. It was almost too much to take. *How could he cheat on such an amazing woman? But what if it's worse than cheating? If Janet's ex thinks he's an asshole on the football pitch, there's a good chance he's like that at home too. What if Emma was right and Kevin is a bully at home? Maybe Abigail isn't worried about being appropriate – maybe she's afraid of her husband?*

Now he was really concerned. He needed to pay

more attention to what she and Emma said and did, and he definitely needed to meet Kevin.

Just as he arrived back at the table with the drinks, Janet stood up to leave. "So, I'll see you both next week at Emma's birthday party. Bye." She gave Henry a sultry smile as she walked away.

"I didn't know it was Emma's birthday soon." His voice was shaky. "She's having a party?"

Abi sighed and reached for her handbag. She fished out a wrinkled envelope and placed it on the table. "I'm so sorry I didn't tell you sooner. I've been carrying Toby's invitation around for two weeks. As much as I want you both to be there, I didn't know whether or not it was appropriate. Kevin will be there."

His body tensed but he tried to act casual. "I can be in the same room as him, Abigail. I promise I won't challenge him to a duel or anything." But after what he'd heard, he was afraid he might have to.

"That's not funny. But of course you should come. I don't know why I hesitated. It's at 1 p.m. in the community centre. Why don't you bring Becca along?"

"What?" The only reason he could think of for bringing Becca was so they would look like a couple.

"I won't be able to talk to you the whole time. I'll have to mingle, and I don't want you to feel lonely. Bring her. I insist! Emma didn't stop talking about her all last night and I know she'd love to come and watch the kids play."

He was still sceptical, but he didn't want to upset her. "OK, I'll see what she says."

"Great. So, did you see that documentary on Ted Hughes last night?"

Henry knew she was trying to change the subject. He suddenly realised she did that a lot when Kevin's name came up. He was sure he was on to something, but he had to tread carefully. He nodded with enthusiasm. "I set it as homework for my A level classes. I thought I was being cool, giving them TV for homework, but they said I was a bigger drag than their parents for making them stay home on a Friday night. Then Tori reminded them they could watch on demand, so it wasn't a big deal."

Abi sat up straight. "I watched it, sir. Do I get an A?"

"No." He grinned. "You get an A star."

The conversation naturally progressed to Sylvia Plath. Henry listened intently as Abi gave a perfect recital of her favourite poem, 'Lady Lazarus'.

It was nearly time to go. Henry gave the kids their two-minute warning. He was watching Abi collect her belongings when he suddenly felt bold. Their chat the day before had cleared the air between them. They had agreed to just be friends, but friends could have lunch together.

"So, are you free for lunch any day during the week?"

She narrowed her eyes at him. "Aren't you back to school?"

"Yes, but they do let me take a lunch break. It's only forty minutes but it's long enough to grab a cup of tea one day before you pick up Emma."

She was really tempted, but the one and only time they had been alone together could easily have spiralled out of control. Maybe they should limit their contact to Saturday mornings at soft play.

"I can't. I'll be busy with preparations for the party. Emma has her heart set on a princess theme. I've got a showstopper cake to bake, I'm making all the decorations and crowns for the kids. I've got to buy and put together the party bags, wrap the pass-the-parcel presents, and Kevin has decided that she will be getting a pony for Christmas and wants her to have riding lessons in advance. Not only do I have to find a good riding school, I've got to source shoes and a hat."

"Um, I think you mean boots and a helmet." He laughed.

"See, I've got so much to do!"

"OK then, we'll do a swap. You meet me on Monday for lunch and I'll help you out with the riding lessons. Google and I will do the legwork. All you'll have to do is pay. Deal?"

She shifted in her seat. She was more than capable of doing it on her own, but a bit of company wouldn't hurt. She nodded. "Lunch it is."

"Great. By the way, isn't a pony a bit extravagant?"

"That's what I said but I was overruled, as usual." She held up her hands to display her rings and Rolex. "You might think I'm spoiled, but Emma is his real princess. He loves her more than anything. Oh – well, you know what I mean." She went quiet. She was desperate for Kevin to love her as much as he loved Emma. She hated being jealous of her own daughter.

Chapter Eleven

Abi and Henry met for a quick bite on Monday at a little café beside his school. But when one of his Year Twelve boys saw them and congratulated Henry on his hot new girlfriend, Abi decided it was too risky to do that again. So, when he suggested they do the same on Tuesday, she suggested that they had a picnic lunch instead. She was waiting in her car at the school gates when the bell rang, and they drove to a nearby park. They didn't mind that it was raining, and were more than happy to eat their sandwiches in the car. After school on Wednesday, Abi asked Glenda to look after Emma and picked Henry up after work. They went to the equestrian shop to collect the gilet and jodhpurs Abi had reserved the night before.

On Thursday evening, Henry picked Toby up from the childminder and they met Abi and Emma for a playdate at a park in the next town. They sat next to each other on a bench and chatted as they watched the children play.

"Oh, I almost forgot. I've got something for you." Abi beamed as she reached into her bag for an envelope which she handed him with excitement.

Remembering the expensive clock she had once threatened to buy him, he took it with caution. "What is this?"

"It's a little thank-you for all your help with the riding stuff. Open it and see." She was bouncing in her seat with excitement.

His mind was racing as he slowly opened it. "You

didn't have to buy me anything."

She blushed. "I didn't … buy you anything."

He pulled a long rectangular item from the envelope. The flowery pattern was vaguely familiar, it was laminated, and there was a hole punched in the top – or was it the bottom? A long piece of material had been pulled through the hole. He thought it looked a bit like a… "Is this a bookmark?"

"Not just *any* bookmark. Do you recognise it?"

"A bit." He screwed up his face.

She tutted. "It's one of your napkins, from the lunch you made me last week. And this…" – she pointed to the material hanging from it – "is the material that was holding together the tea towel bundle you bought at the outlet village. It was far too pretty to throw away. I know it's primitive, but I thought you might like it."

He couldn't believe it. It was so personal and sentimental. He'd treasure it. "I love it. I can't believe you made this for me." He looked into her eyes; they were full of excitement. He'd never seen her looking so beautiful, and he'd never wanted to kiss her more. The week had been fantastic … like a string of great dates. OK, they weren't dates in the traditional sense, but it didn't matter what they did, as long as they were together. He took her hand and squeezed it and was amazed when she didn't pull away. And when she locked fingers with him, all the promises he made over the quiche the week before were forgotten. He simply couldn't stop himself from whispering, "I really want to kiss you, Abigail."

The words made her pulse quicken. She wanted to kiss him too, desperately. But she fixed her eyes on her knees and prayed he couldn't see them shaking. Terrified that she was even contemplating it, she returned her gaze to him and saw his cheeks were flushed. She had a quick look around the park. No one knew them and no one was even watching. It was just a kiss. What could it hurt? She was inching closer to him when the shrill music of the ice-cream van made her jump.

"Ice cream!" She dropped his hand and, without giving him a second look, hurried off to the ice-cream van.

He let out a long sigh and buried his head in his hands. How had that nearly just happened? He couldn't believe he'd stepped over the line he had so clearly drawn for himself. His heart was in his mouth. He'd nearly kissed her but, more importantly, she'd nearly kissed him. He was so caught up in the moment that he didn't even notice the woman storming towards him.

"Is the one with the pigtails yours?" she snapped.

He looked up to find her pointing at Emma. He glanced over at Abi, who was in conversation with the ice-cream man, then back at the woman. "Erm, yes. She's mine."

"You need to teach your daughter some manners. She just *body-shamed* mine." She was furious.

He stood up to face her. "Body-shamed?"

"It's when—"

"Yes. I know what it is." He sighed. Unfortunately, he knew exactly what it was – half the kids at his school were at it. "What I meant was, she couldn't have. She's only four years old."

"She did! My daughter was eating a chocolate bar and yours told her not to. Said 'she didn't need the extra weight'. Children her age learn that sort of stuff at home. What kind of a father are you?" She pointed her finger in his face.

Henry took a step backward. "I'm sorry that it happened. I'll definitely talk to her. But there's no need for such hostility." He called over to Emma. "Emma, come here *now*." He beckoned her.

Emma came running over to him, looking as if butter wouldn't melt in her mouth. She flashed an innocent smile at the woman, who glared at her in return.

The woman, obviously lingering to watch the scolding, shifted her glance between Henry and Emma. "Well?"

"Well. I can handle it from here. Sorry again," Henry said, with the authority only a teacher of rowdy teenagers could command. The woman stormed off.

"Emma, what did you say to that girl?"

"I told her not to eat chocolate because it will make her fat. She doesn't need the extra weight."

"Why on earth would you say such a thing?"

"To be nice."

"Nice?"

"Yes. Daddy says it to Mummy all the time."

Henry gritted his teeth. "That's not nice. And your mummy's not fat, sweetie."

"Only because Daddy stops her eating. He says if he didn't, her ass would be the size of a house and the last thing he needs is a fat wife." She held out her hands as if it was a fact.

He couldn't believe his ears. He wasn't sure which was worse, the fact that Kevin said those things, or that Emma thought it was natural. "Emma, those are not nice things to say. I won't tell your mummy that you said them, but you have to promise me that you'll never say anything like that again."

She gave him her most precious smile. "I promise,

Henry. But 'imp-com-py-tent' is a nice thing to say, isn't it?"

"Why do you ask, sweetie?"

"Because Daddy says that to Mummy all the time too."

Now his blood was boiling. What the hell was that man talking about? Abigail was perfect, but that wasn't even the point. What sort of man says those things about his own wife, and in front of their child? His head was spinning as he saw Abi approaching with three ice creams. He tried to pull himself together. He couldn't talk to her about this at the park. He needed time to think of the best way to approach it. He decided to keep his conversation with Emma to himself for now.

Abi announced the ice creams and Toby came running. She offered the third one to Henry, who still looked flushed. "I'm sorry about before. I don't know what I was thinking. Maybe this will cool you down."

He forced a laugh as he took the third ice cream. "Aren't you having one?"

"I shouldn't. I'm trying to be good. Waistband is getting a little tight." She adjusted her coat.

He made sure she noticed him looking her up and down. "There's nothing wrong with your waist, Abigail. You look beautiful. You always look beautiful."

She shifted from foot to foot but returned a little smile. "We should go after this. I've got a busy day baking tomorrow."

"Do you need any help?"

"You bake?"

"No, but I've been baked."

She drew a sharp breath. "Hopefully not at school."

"Relax – in uni. I can come over after school and

help you."

That wasn't the worst idea in the world. She'd love his company, and it was Friday. Kevin didn't come home on Fridays. He'd never miss an after-work drinking session. But they'd been very close to ending up in bed when they'd been alone at his flat, and just now, they'd nearly kissed. Maybe it wasn't a good idea to have Henry at her house. Best to keep things above board. "No. It's OK. I've got it all planned out; I just need to focus tomorrow. I want Emma's party to be perfect."

"Oh, about that. Becca can't come. She asked me to pass on her apologies."

The look on Abi's face confirmed his suspicions about Becca's invite. Abi didn't want a single man at the party in case her husband questioned it. As much as he wanted to be there to meet Kevin, he didn't want to cause Abi any upset at her daughter's birthday party. He'd figure out another way.

"It's OK, Toby and I will take a rain check. I don't want to make things awkward for you."

"Thank you, Henry," she said quietly. She really wanted him to be there. Emma would want Toby there too – and it was her special day. Maybe there was a way they could come to the party, as long as Henry stayed away from Kevin. "I do want you both to come. Just—"

"Just don't talk to you too much, and stay away from Kevin?"

She ran her hand down his arm. "If you don't mind."

"How could I be OK with not talking to you? I'll do it, but only because that's what you want me to do. I'd do anything for you, Abigail. You know that, don't you?"

She looked confused. "Yes…"

"And if you ever wanted to talk to me, about anything, you know I'm here for you. Don't you?"

"Yes. Henry, what's going on? You're making me nervous."

"Nothing, and I didn't mean to make you nervous. We'd better get you home. It's getting late."

She checked her watch. It *was* late. She touched the scar on her temple. Kevin would be home soon, and he wouldn't be happy if dinner wasn't on the table.

Chapter Twelve

The next morning, Emma ran through the school gates and joined her friends. After having a brief chat with some of the other mums, Abi hurried back to the car. She had a lot to do for the party the next day, but she had made a list the night before and had everything all planned out.

After stopping four times to collect supplies, she arrived back at the house and started party preparations. No sooner had she poured the cake mixture into the moulds and placed them in the oven than her mind turned to Henry. This was the first day that week that she hadn't seen him. To make matters worse, they were going to miss their standing date at soft play because of Emma's party. She was glad he was coming, but she wouldn't be able to speak to him as much as she wanted. Then she remembered she had his mobile number. She ran upstairs to Emma's bedroom and hunted for the phonics book. She brought it back downstairs then sat at the kitchen table and tried to come up with an excuse to text him. A confirmation of the party time and location – that would do. After she had sent the text, she spent the next fifteen minutes checking her phone to see if he had replied before realising that he would be in class and unable to use his phone. She glanced at the clock. It was only ten minutes until his lunchtime.

Eleven minutes later, she received a reply. Not wanting to seem over-eager, she waited for twenty-five minutes before replying. He replied immediately and they ended up texting back and forth for the rest of the afternoon. She gave him regular updates on the party preparations and he always replied with a cute emoji and lots of praise for her hard work.

After school, Emma was at the kitchen table doing homework, eager to get it out of the way so she could enjoy her birthday weekend. Abi had just finished cleaning up after baking and crafting when she thought about dinner. She was exhausted and the kitchen was spotless; she didn't want to create a new mess by cooking. As it was Friday, and Kevin didn't come home for dinner on Fridays, Abi decided to take Emma to McDonald's as a pre-birthday treat. She texted Henry, just to let him know, and he replied quickly. He said it was a huge coincidence because he had suggested the very same to Toby, and wouldn't it be a further coincidence if they all turned up at the McDonald's beside the cinema at exactly six o'clock?

At exactly six o'clock, Abi and Emma arrived at the McDonald's beside the cinema. As they walked in, Emma spotted Toby at the counter with Henry and ran over to them.

"Hi!" she said excitedly, wrapping her arms around Henry's leg.

"What are you doing here, sweetie?" He ruffled her hair and gave Abi a knowing glance.

"It's a birthday treat. What are you doing here? I hope it's not fast food every night you have Toby?" Abi chided with a smirk.

"No! I'm just tired after a busy week. I'll have you know I'm a good cook. You should taste my quiche."

"I'm sure it's delicious." Abi tried hard not to blush and pointed over to Emma and Toby, who had already claimed a table for four. "Looks like the children would like to sit together. I suppose you're stuck with me."

Henry shuffled his feet. "I can think of worse things on a Friday night."

***

After Abi had read Emma a story and tucked her into bed, she relaxed in a warm bubble bath with a cold glass of wine. The past week had been amazing. She'd spent so much time with Henry – and had enjoyed every minute of it. She couldn't remember the last time she had been out on a Friday night. Although Friday evening at a fast food restaurant was very different to her nights out before she'd married. Her thoughts turned to Kevin. He went out every Friday night with his friends, and most Saturday nights. There was no reason for her to feel guilty about doing the same.

Abi settled down in bed. Everything was ready for the party the next day, and she was really looking forward to it. She was just setting the alarm on her phone when she panicked. She didn't know whether Kevin ever checked her phone or read her text messages but, if he did, he wouldn't be too happy to find out she'd been texting another man. Just to be on the safe side, she read the day's texts from Henry again, deleted them and then his number. She could always retrieve it from the phonics book at any time. She turned off the light and settled down to sleep, hoping to dream about Henry.

But that was not to be.

Kevin stumbled into the bedroom at half past two and fell onto the bed beside Abi. "Abs," he groaned, then belched. He was stinking drunk.

He rubbed her arm. "Abs … wake up."

Still nothing. He tapped her arm repeatedly until she began to stir. When the smell of beer hit her nose, she sat bolt upright, panicking.

"What is it, Kevin? Is everything OK?"

"No, s'not." He sounded pathetic. "Got kebab sauce on my jeans."

She let out a long sigh and lay back down. "That's OK. I'll see to them in the morning."

"Abs, if you really loved me, you'd see to them now," he begged. "They're my favourite…"

"In the morning, Kevin."

He glared at her. When she still didn't get up, he pulled the duvet off her. "Don't be so goddamn lazy! Get downstairs, Fat Abs, and do it now. And mop the floor. My beer got spilt."

His tone was familiar. She'd learned it was best to do as he said, otherwise she'd get the silent treatment for the next few days. She jumped out of bed and pulled on her dressing gown.

"Oh, and that cake…" He pretended to gag. "Yuk."

The cake! She hurried downstairs and ran through the kitchen into the utility room, where she'd put the cake for safekeeping. She held her breath and turned on the light. Tears began to stream down her face when she saw the once perfect pink castle. Kevin had taken a huge bite out of one of the turrets. The little pony she had constructed from icing had had its leg bitten off, and there were fingerprints in her icing moat. That cake had taken her weeks of planning and experimenting, and a whole day to put together.

It was ruined.

She sat down on the floor of the utility room, buried her head in her hands and sobbed uncontrollably. It was a few minutes before she could summon up the courage to look at the cake again. After a closer inspection she decided it wasn't that bad after all. There had been some leftover cake mixture, but instead of throwing it away she had made half a dozen cupcakes to take to her mother. If she scraped the cream off one, she could probably use it to plug the hole in the turret. She could make some more icing and spread it over the joins. There was a block of marzipan left that she could use to make a new leg for the pony. And the fingerprints in the moat could be turned into waves.

As she dried her tears and prepared herself for the task ahead, her relief turned to anger. *How could he have done this to Emma's cake? He knows how much effort I've made – he was more than happy to eat the practice cakes! And he knows how much this cake means to Emma. How would he feel if something he loved got destroyed? Wait … where are his jeans?* She marched back into the kitchen and found them on the floor beside the table. She inspected the stain, which was just a tiny splash of sauce on one leg. Luckily, she had the very thing to get rid of it.

After she'd finished with the jeans, repaired the cake, mopped the kitchen floor and locked the front door, she went back upstairs. She went into the bedroom, which stank of beer, and found Kevin passed out on top of the duvet, half dressed. She turned off the light and went into the guest bedroom – not that she was allowed to have guests any more. Exhausted and anxious, she climbed into bed. Kevin would go mad if he realised she was in there, not by his side as a good wife should be. But she figured it would be OK: he was far too drunk to notice and she would be up hours before him in the morning.

She stared at the ceiling and tried to figure out what had gone wrong with her life. She did everything she could to make Kevin happy. But nothing was ever good enough. Maybe she was a failure as a wife and a mother. Her thoughts turned to her own mother. Even though she had been widowed young and had to balance parenting two teenage daughters and a full-time job, Abi and her sister had a happy childhood and never went without. Abi was grateful that, since her mother's stroke, Kevin had paid for her care at the best private nursing home in town. She was so well treated there. Abi tried to reason with herself. The only thing wrong in her life was her, and she was luckier than most people. She was just being selfish. So what if Kevin wasn't a doting husband? She hadn't given him any reason to be. He provided for her and their daughter, and apart from the occasional reminder when he thought Abi was being ungrateful, he was happy to pay for her mum's care too. That was what was important – family. And it was probably normal that, after a few years of marriage and with a child to raise, the romance had worn off. The only way for things to change would be if *she* changed. She had to try harder at her marriage, and she definitely had to rethink her relationship with Henry. What was she doing? She had tried to pretend that she only saw him because the children got on so well together, but that wasn't true. She loved every minute she spent with him. They had got very close to overstepping the line the day before, and that couldn't happen again. She couldn't risk her marriage by having an affair, and she wasn't being fair to Henry. She knew she was the reason he wasn't dating. He wanted to get married again, have more children. She was holding him back.

With a heavy heart, she decided she had to let Henry go. She'd tell him on Monday.

Chapter Thirteen

Abi was on edge preparing the breakfast. Adrenaline fuelled by rage had made her act out the night before, but now she regretted it. What had she been thinking? Kevin would go mad when he saw his jeans, but there was no way to undo what she'd done and she wasn't going to beg for forgiveness.

Not this time.

Ruining Emma's birthday cake was unforgivable. She had accepted that he didn't appreciate everything she did for him, but Emma was just a child. His child. He should want her to be happy. Emma shouldn't have to earn his love, like Abi did.

Kevin was quieter than usual when he finally came down to the kitchen. Emma was already at the table, eating. He pulled out the chair opposite and sat down. He sank his head into his hands, looking green.

"Good morning, Kevin," Abi said politely. She shooed his elbows off the table and placed his usual full English in front of him. Then poured him some tea.

He grunted and picked up his cutlery.

She watched him as he ate, shovelling forkful after forkful into his mouth. Egg yolk ran down his chin. He wiped it away with the back of his hand, which he then wiped on his pyjama bottoms. Despite his fancy clothes and huge bank balance, he was an animal. Emma had better table manners. Abi wasn't sure if her feelings were caused by residual anger from the night before or if she actually hated him. Before she spoke, she took a deep breath to summon her courage. "That stain was a little tricky, honey, but I got it out." She handed him the perfect circle she'd cut from his jeans.

He squinted at it, then at her. Then he spotted his destroyed jeans hanging over the chair and the perfectly repaired cake sitting on the worktop. He set down his cutlery and looked at Emma.

"Why don't you go upstairs and get dressed, princess?"

"Yes, honey. I've left out your favourite jumper and a nice pair of leggings for you."

He sneered. "Emma, I've told you before not to let Mummy dress you like a boy. Why don't you pick out a nice dress to wear today? My princess has to look lovely for her party."

"OK, Daddy." Emma ran off upstairs.

He held up the denim circle. "I didn't realise you were so petty, Abs."

"I couldn't help it. How could you do that to Emma's cake?" she asked quietly.

"I had to taste it before you served it at the party today. I didn't want to be embarrassed in front of everyone if it tasted like shit. By some miracle it was OK – just – so you can serve it. But I'm sick of you not listening to me. Next time, get one from the patisserie like I told you to, no matter what the cost. I don't want my daughter's friends laughing at her because her cake is homemade. Or their parents thinking we can't afford a proper one."

"A *proper* one? That cake is as good as any bakery would make. And for the record, I don't care what people think."

He gestured to her outfit. "That's obvious."

She gasped and looked down at her new designer blouse and Capri trousers. The saleswoman in the boutique had told her she looked stunning. She should have realised that people will say anything when they're on commission. Embarrassed, she rushed out of the kitchen and trudged upstairs to get changed.

He shouted after her. "And put some make-up on!"

**

Henry marvelled at the enormous pink castle. There was a moat, turrets, flags and a little icing character that looked like Emma on a pony waving to little icing subjects. He wondered why Abi had gone to all the bother when she had more than enough money to buy a fancy cake. She was really pulling out all the stops for Emma.

"It really is a showstopper."

"Thank you. It took weeks of planning and then all day to put together. But it was worth every minute to see the look on her little face." Abi beamed. "She was delighted."

"And I'm very impressed. If I was Paul Hollywood, I would make you Star Baker."

"How do you know Paul Hollywood?"

"Um, Becca used to watch *Bake Off*."

"And I'm guessing that you still do."

He shrugged. "I'm invested in it."

She laughed and pointed to the other parents. "Shouldn't you mingle?"

"I've hardly talked to you. Surely you can give me a minute of your time."

When she tutted then rolled her eyes, he knew he'd hit a nerve. "Are you OK?" he asked gently.

"I'm fine." But she didn't sound fine. Henry had

been married; he knew full well that was code. He tilted his head and made a funny face at her until she cracked a smile.

"I'm just tired. I was so busy with the cake yesterday and I didn't sleep very well last night."

"You were probably too excited about the party. But it all looks great. You look great too." He winked.

"Don't." She looked over his shoulder at Kevin, who was standing at the back of the room talking to some of the dads.

Henry glanced behind him and saw four men at the back of the room. He knew straight away which was Kevin. He was the best dressed – and the one doing all the talking. There was something about his demeanour that Henry immediately disliked.

"Don't worry. I promised I'd stay away from Kevin and I will. Which one is he?"

She drew a sharp breath. "The one who just noticed us talking and is on his way over."

It was time to make himself scarce. "I'll leave you to it. This is a great party, by the way. Emma is a very lucky little girl." Then he whispered, "Will I see you on Monday for lunch?"

Her heart sank. She was dreading Monday, but she had to let Henry go. She nodded.

Henry turned. As he walked away, he overheard Kevin ask, "Who was that man you were just talking to?"

"Oh, I can't remember his name. I speak to his wife at drop-off and pick-up, but she couldn't make it, so he brought their son instead."

Kevin glared at Henry. "He has a wife? He looks gay."

She sighed. Kevin always said that about men he

thought were better-looking than he was. He hated not being the most sought-after man in the room.

"John says he's a teacher at his son's school. Teaches English. That proves he's gay. I'll bet he does housework too. What a pussy."

Henry walked away, clenching his fists. He promised Abi he wouldn't talk to Kevin, but he hadn't promised he wouldn't talk *about* Kevin. He saw a group of women by the bouncy castle and recognised one of the women he'd met at Abi's house and Maggie, the head of the PTA. They all stopped talking and stared at him as he joined them. He felt a little objectified.

One of the women, who was wearing a low-cut red top, looked at him like she was about to undress for him right then and there. "Whose are you?" she purred, tugging on the drawstring of his hoodie.

The woman from Abi's house intervened. "This is Henry – he's a friend of Abi's. Hi, Henry. It's lovely to see you again."

"Hi, yes, you too. Marie, isn't it?"

"You remembered."

He gave his most charming smile. "How could I forget? This is a great party, ladies, isn't it?"

"I wouldn't have expected anything less. Abi always excels herself." Maggie looked longingly at Abi. "I envy her. She always looks perfect, her house is amazing, and that husband of hers is delicious."

"Cut it out, Maggie. He's a pig," Marie scolded. "She's gone to all this effort for this party and he hasn't even lifted a finger. I overheard him saying he wished he was playing football."

"He's just not the kids' birthday party type. He's more of a man's man," Maggie defended him.

"You mean he's more of a *ladies'* man," the woman in the red top offered.

Suddenly interested, Henry held his hand out for her to shake. "I'm sorry, I haven't had the pleasure."

"I'm Nikki, and you can have my pleasure any time."

Henry winced. So, Janet wasn't the only one who knew about Kevin and his women. "Are you guys saying Abi's husband cheats?"

"No, Henry. We're not," Marie said quickly.

"They're just rumours," Maggie agreed.

"Come on, guys. I told you I've seen it with my own eyes. He's a cheat. And a nasty, arrogant prick. He's always getting drunk and thrown out of bars in town. The poor girl has no idea."

They all looked sympathetically at Abi, who was busy being the perfect hostess. Henry could feel his blood starting to boil again. "Has anybody talked to her about it?"

They all shook their heads vigorously. "No. Never get involved in someone's marriage," Marie offered.

"It never ends well," Maggie agreed.

"Best to leave it, Henry," Nikki advised. "No one wants to hear bad news about their marriage. Abi's happy in her own little world. It's best just to let her be."

But Henry had seen and heard enough evidence to suspect that she couldn't possibly be happy. She was probably far from it. His head was spinning. He had to excuse himself from the group.

He was about to go back to Abi to see if she needed any help when he spotted Glenda feeding her baby at the side of the room. She was Abi's best friend – maybe she knew what was going on.

"Hi Glenda, hi precious." He waved to the baby, who glared at him. He grimaced. "I'm told the ladies love me … not all of them, apparently."

Glenda laughed. "Hi Henry. You look well."

"You too. This is a great party, isn't it?"

"Yes. Abi always goes the extra mile where Emma is concerned."

"Doesn't look like Kevin helps out much."

"He rarely does." Her harsh tone told Henry that she wasn't overly fond of Kevin. "He's a complete chauvinist. He earns the money, therefore she has to do everything else."

"You must know him well."

"Not really. When she met him, we thought he was great. My husband and I used to hang out with them all the time. But once they were married it was a different story. We saw him and Abi less and less, then we just saw Abi. Then we saw less of Abi." She looked archly at Henry. "I'm surprised she let you come. Kevin gets very jealous if he sees her talking to another man. He made her give up her job as soon as they were married. Just because they met when she showed him a house, he thinks she's going to jump into bed with every guy she meets at work." She narrowed her eyes at Kevin. "He's got a cheek. She's the only one who's loyal to wedding vows in that marriage."

"Tell me about it," he said under his breath.

"What?"

"Nothing. Have you ever talked to her about his cheating?"

"Yes. Once, a year or so ago. She got defensive and called me jealous. She didn't speak to me for two months. Then I had to pretend I'd got it wrong and beg for her forgiveness. But I wish cheating was the worst of it. He's a real control freak. He tells her what to wear and how to behave. If I've heard him tell her to 'be appropriate' once, I've heard it a million times. And he's stripped her of her confidence."

"What? I think she's confident."

"She's not the same Abi I grew up with. When she first got married, she started dressing differently. No more high street fashion; she became very high end. When I asked her about it, she said Kevin had 'suggested' she treat herself to nicer clothes, show off some of the money he was making. The next 'suggestion' was that she give up her job. I was a little taken aback because she loved her job and was really good at it. And it was such a bonus that we could work together again. But she seemed happy parading around, spending money – she was having the time of her life. I admit I was a little jealous at first, but not in a spiteful way. I was happy for her. She seemed like she was really enjoying married life." She frowned.

Henry looked concerned.

"It was when she got pregnant with Emma that I began to suspect that things weren't right. Of course Abi had stopped drinking, so she wasn't that interested in nights out any more. Instead she was busy making plans for the baby, the nursery, et cetera. People around town were starting to get over Kevin's 'big man' routine and everyone was focused on Abi. Suddenly Kevin wasn't the centre of attention any more, and he hated that. One night, Abi rang me, distraught. Crying down the phone. He hadn't come home, and she was worried that something awful had happened to him. He turned up the next day with a ridiculous story about how he got caught up in a conference and stayed in London. His mobile died and he couldn't remember her number. He said he'd tried ringing the house, but she didn't pick up. Tried to turn it around on her. Where was she if she wasn't at home to answer his call? I'm sure that's when the cheating started. I couldn't remember him ever going on a business trip before that, then suddenly he was away all the time." Glenda sighed and looked over at Abi. "Then the worst thing of all happened. Abi was nearly eight months pregnant when her mother had a major stroke. She was left incapacitated and needed full-time care. Abi and her sister Evelyn were devastated. Their dad died in a car accident when Abi was ten and she felt like she'd lost her mother too, just when she needed her most."

Henry's heart sank. He and Abi had talked about their childhoods many times, but he had no idea that her father was dead or that her mother was ill. Some friend he was.

"Abi's health really suffered. Her blood pressure went through the roof and her doctor was worried about her and the baby so he admitted her to hospital for the last few weeks. That was Kevin's time to shine again. He took over organising everything and relished all the attention he got. He fussed over Abi at the hospital and arranged for her mother to move to St James's and paid for her care there. Everyone thought he was a hero – so devoted to his wife and even taking care of her sick mother. There were a few rumours that Kevin had a woman or two at the house when Abi was in hospital—"

"He cheated on her while she was in hospital, pregnant?"

"No one wanted to believe that, so everyone shrugged it off. There had to be another explanation. It was a cleaner or a decorator. And then when Emma was born, Abi couldn't cope. She was still in shock about her mum's condition and was suffering from postnatal depression – she wouldn't admit it, but it was obvious. Kevin did nothing to help her. In fact, he did the opposite – actually encouraged her to stay in bed and not seek help. He got his mum, Beverly, to come and stay at their house for a few weeks. Beverly made all the decisions about looking after Emma. Kevin said she'd had three children so she knew what she was doing, unlike Abi, who couldn't even look after herself, never mind a baby. I didn't see her for about three weeks. Every time I rang her mobile, Beverly or Kevin answered and fobbed me off by saying she was asleep or in the bath. I went to the house a couple of times and was told she didn't want visitors. I got really concerned about her and phoned her sister, Evelyn. She hadn't heard much from Abi either, so she went around there and wouldn't take no for an answer. She took control. She got Abi up and dressed and took her and Emma to see their mother. She had settled in well at the nursing home. The visit really lifted Abi's spirits. Evelyn sent Kevin's mum home and stayed at the house for a few days. She made sure Abi got up and out every day and made sure she had plenty of time with Emma. She also called Abi's GP and arranged for some emotional support – all the things that Kevin should have done. Things slowly got back to normal, but it was a new normal. Abi had lost her confidence. I don't think she's ever fully recovered."

Henry couldn't believe what he was hearing. He had no idea what she'd been through. He felt awful. All he wanted to do was go to Abi and comfort her.

Glenda seemed to notice his turmoil. "I've seen flickers of the old Abi recently, since she met you. Is there something going on between you two?"

"No! What makes you say that?"

"I have eyes. I saw the way you looked at each other last week, and there's been talk that you've been spotted together around town a few times."

I thought we'd been discreet. "It's nothing. We're just friends, honestly."

"Well, you'd better be careful. I wouldn't want to be around if Kevin finds out you've been seeing so much of each other. 'Just friends' or not."

"What's that supposed to mean? Do you think he'd be violent?"

"I've heard he's got a reputation for threatening behaviour at work. In football he's sent off all the time for dirty tackling. And at the pub he's been in more than a few brawls."

"Do you think he's violent … towards Abi?"

Glenda looked over at Abi and sighed. "She's never said anything, and I've never seen any evidence of it, but I wouldn't be surprised. He does control her, I know that for sure. I don't know what to do for the best, so I just bite my tongue and try to be a good friend. If she fell out with me again, she'd have no one to talk to."

"She has me now."

Glenda raised an eyebrow.

He tried to reassure her. "That wasn't a dig. You're her best friend and she needs you. I'll talk to her, even if it means she doesn't speak to me again."

"She's fragile. Be gentle with her."

Henry was one of the last to leave. He watched as Abi handed out party bags to the children. Just as he was about to approach with Toby, Kevin joined Abi. Henry nudged Toby. "You go, and don't forget to say thank you."

Toby ran up to Abi and threw his arms around her. "Thank you, Abi."

"You're welcome, cutie." As she handed the party bag to Toby, she looked over at Henry and gave him a half smile. He smiled back then took Toby's hand and headed to the door.

He was strapping Toby into his car seat when Toby screamed, "*Puddles!* Daddy, I forgot Puddles!" Puddles was Toby's favourite teddy bear. Becca had always threatened Henry with castration if Puddles got lost on his watch.

"OK, you stay put. I'll get him." Henry groaned as he closed the car door, locked it and ran back into the community centre. Puddles was on the floor, just outside the door to the large hall. Henry couldn't help but overhear a conversation that was going on inside.

"... and at least some of the women made a bit of effort with their appearance. Shame about their host."

Henry peered in through the window and saw Emma run into her daddy's arms.

"Well, princess, did you enjoy your party?"

"Yes, Daddy. Thank you for missing football for it."

"That's OK – anything for my princess. You and Mummy can drop me at the Red Lion on your way home."

"Actually, Kev, we were going to go to Glenda's for tea and some more cake."

"Straight home, Abs," he instructed. "You've done enough socialising for today and the last thing you need is more cake. I'll be calling the house to make sure you're there. And don't forget you have to get me some new jeans. Actually, I think I'll need two pairs. Get it sorted. And I mean today, not next week. Got it?"

She turned away to pack some presents into a box.

"I said, have you got that?" he snapped.

"Yes, Kevin." Her shoulders slumped and she looked defeated.

It took all Henry's willpower not to march into the hall and confront Kevin. But he knew that would probably just add fuel to the fire. He needed to get Abi alone.

***

Henry felt sick for the rest of the weekend. He paced his flat, thinking about everything he had seen and heard about Kevin. He berated himself. How could he not have seen that Abi was in an abusive relationship? He'd had loads of training at work on how to recognise the signs of domestic abuse – specifically in children, but most of the signs were the same – yet nothing had alerted him until Becca had raised a red flag. He didn't have any evidence to suggest that Kevin was physically abusive, but he was certainly possessive and controlling. Unfortunately, Henry knew that men like that had the tendency to turn violent if they felt their control over their partner was slipping. Why hadn't he joined the dots sooner? he thought, distraught. It was probably because Abigail didn't look like someone who was being abused. She was beautiful and well dressed. She was kind and always seemed happy. He was ashamed those things had distracted him. He was just as bad as the majority of people who assumed that all abuse was physical. He hadn't paid too much attention to her half-eaten scones, constant putting herself down and her worries about what people thought of her — even her reluctance to be seen in public with him. He was desperate to talk to her, but where? He couldn't do it in front of Emma, and what if Kevin came back? He'd have to wait until Monday to speak to Abi.

If he could last that long.

He felt so guilty that he'd failed her.

Chapter Fourteen

Henry thought Monday morning would never come. He drove to Richmond Hill and parked his car in front of Abi's house. His stomach was in knots as he went over in his head what he'd been practising all weekend. He was summoning up the courage to get out of the car when he saw Abi driving towards him. He got out of the car as she pulled into her driveway.

She practically abandoned the car and jumped out to meet him as he walked through the gate. "What are you doing here?" she snapped. "Any why aren't you at work?"

"I phoned in sick."

Her anger quickly turned to concern. "Sick? Are you OK?"

"I need to talk to you. Let's go inside." He took a step towards the front door. She grabbed his arm.

"No! What would the neighbours think?"

"I don't care."

"I do." She looked around cautiously.

His suspicions had been confirmed. Why had it taken him so long to put the pieces together? She was really afraid that Kevin might find out about him being at the house. "OK, I'll go, but I want you to come round to my flat in half an hour."

"I can't just go gallivanting. I've got stuff to do."

"Please, Abigail. If you don't come, I'll just come back here again. Please say you'll meet me there in half an hour?"

"OK. But what is this about? Why did you come

here?"

"We need to talk."

"About what?"

"Don't worry," he said with a smile, "everything is going to be OK." He walked back to his car.

Her heart was pounding. He wouldn't think it was OK after what she had to tell him. She didn't know if she was more worried about what he was going to say, or what she was preparing to tell him.

***

Henry paced the living-room floor while he waited for Abi. The sound of the doorbell made him jump. He hurried to the door and buzzed Abi up to his flat. He was waiting at the door when the lift opened.

"OK. I'm here. What's so important that it couldn't wait until this afternoon?"

"The kettle has just boiled. Would you like a cup of tea?"

She walked past him into the living room. "No. What I would like is for you to tell me why I'm here."

"Please sit down."

She sat on the edge of the sofa. He joined her and reached for her hand. Reluctantly she let him take it, then squinted at him. "Henry, you're pale. Are you sure you're not sick?"

"I haven't slept." His heart was pounding. "This isn't going to be an easy conversation, for either of us."

Oh my God. Is he going to tell me he loves me? She pulled her hand from his. "Henry, I hope this isn't what I think it is. We're friends. Nothing more. We can't be."

He hung his head. "I know. And it's because we're

friends that I need to talk to you. I need to make sure that you're OK."

"Of course I'm OK. But I'm also confused."

"I'm sorry. I'm not handling this very well." He took her hand again. "I want you to know that I'm here for you and that you can tell me anything."

"I wish you would tell me what this is about."

"All right. I want to ask you if everything is OK at home?"

"Everything's fine. Why do you ask?"

"Because I'm worried about you, Abigail."

"Why are you worried?"

"It's just … I've … noticed things…"

"What kind of things?"

"Is everything OK between you and Kevin?"

She gave a nervous laugh. "Yes."

"Are you sure?"

She gritted her teeth. "Yes."

He looked uncertain. "I don't think Kevin is treating you very well."

"I don't know what you're talking about."

"I've seen and heard things I don't like. And it's not just me. I spoke to some of your friends at Emma's party. They told me lots of things about Kevin that I didn't like."

She recoiled. "You've been talking about me behind my back?"

"Only because I'm worried about you."

"All right. So, what have my so-called friends been saying about me?"

"That your husband isn't a very nice man."

"Don't be ridiculous – everyone loves Kevin," she said defensively. "And I don't mean to be rude, but you're hardly objective."

He took a deep breath before he continued. "And they say that he's cheating on you."

Her jaw dropped. "He's what?"

"I'm so sorry, Abigail. They've all heard rumours, and Nikki says she's actually seen it."

"Nikki?" She scoffed. "People in glass houses shouldn't throw stones."

"It wasn't just Nikki. And it's not just the cheating. They all say that Kevin is aggressive, and he can get violent, especially when he's been drinking."

"Oh, I see what this is." She pointed her finger at him. "You're angry because I won't sleep with you. You're making things up about my husband so I'll jump into bed with you."

"That's not what this is. I've been talking to Glenda, and—"

"Glenda?" Her lip quivered. "You've talked to Glenda about me?"

"We're really worried about you, Abigail. She told me some worrying things about Kevin. I want you to get away from him."

"Glenda is just jealous; she always has been. And you, making up these lies, you're pathetic."

"I'm not the pathetic one! That would be Kevin. He's got the most amazing, beautiful woman in the world and he treats you like crap."

"He doesn't treat me like crap."

"Why are you defending him? What hold does he have on you?"

"Hold? He's my husband."

"Abigail, he's controlling you."

"He's not controlling me. He's protective."

"It's a very fine line."

"What do you mean, a fine line?" She realised she

had begun to shout so she took a breath and tried to calm herself down. "Henry, my marriage is fine. If anything, we're going through a bit of a bad patch. But it's temporary. It'll get better."

"What sort of bad patch?"

She realised she'd said too much and tried to backtrack. "It's nothing."

"I don't think it's nothing. I've noticed things, heard things, and so have your friends. I can't believe how long it took me to put all the pieces together. All the signs are there."

She squinted at him. "Signs of what?"

"Signs of domestic abuse."

"I beg your pardon? Kevin has never laid a finger on me."

He held his hands up in defence. "OK. I believe you. But abuse isn't always physical. It can be emotional or psychological."

"Oh, because he says some mean things to me, that's abuse?"

He clenched his fists. "It can be. What sort of mean things does he say?"

She looked down at the ground and didn't answer.

"He is controlling, isn't he? He tells you what to do and what not to do. How to behave. Who to talk to. Does he put you down and make you feel worthless?"

Off the top of her head, she could come up with a dozen examples for each of the things he had just said, but she shook her head. "No."

He looked her in the eye. "I believed you when you said he didn't touch you, but I know you're lying now."

She held her composure. "I'm not lying."

"Emma has also been saying some things about the way he treats you."

Her jaw dropped. "Now you're trying to use my child to turn me against my husband? I'd call *that* emotional abuse."

"I'm sorry, but I'm worried about you and Emma."

"There's no need to be worried. They're just words. He gets angry sometimes because he's under so much stress at work."

His heart sank. He knew that physical abuse was often preceded by more subtle abuse. "I'm worried that words are just the start of it. What if it escalates?"

"Escalates? Into what?"

"Physical violence."

Reflexively, she touched the small scar on her temple. "Don't be ridiculous. Kevin would never hurt me."

"You have to be one hundred per cent sure about that. You could be in danger, and Emma too."

She sighed. "Kevin is a good man. A hard worker. A good father. He loves Emma more than anything – he would never hurt her, not even emotionally."

"I bet he loved you like that once. I bet then he never intended hurting you, not even emotionally." He took her hand. "Please let me take you home to get your things. We'll pick up Emma from school and I'll take you anywhere you want to go. I need to make sure that you're safe. It could be a matter of time before he takes the next step."

She pulled her hand from his. "How dare you? I can't believe that you, of all people, are trying to give me marriage advice. Your own wife couldn't wait to get rid of you so she could jump into bed with your best friend."

That was the worst thing he'd ever heard her say, but he tried not to take it to heart. He tried to stay calm. "I'm not trying to break up your marriage because I want you for myself. I want you to be safe – to be as far away from that man as possible. Even if it means I never see you again."

"You just got your wish." She grabbed her bag. "If I see you anywhere near my house or my daughter again, I'll call the police and tell them you're harassing us. That wouldn't look too good for you at school. Would it? Have a nice life, Henry." She tried to storm past him but in a desperate attempt to stop her, he grabbed her by the arm.

"Abigail. Please!"

She glared at him and then at his hand on her arm. He removed it immediately and took a step backwards.

"That is more abuse than my husband has ever subjected me to. And I thought *he* was meant to be the violent one." She pushed past him and hurried out of the flat.

He flinched when the door slammed behind her. *What have I done? Why did I grab her? I couldn't have made a bigger mistake. I have to make it right.* He bolted for the door and made it out into the corridor just as the lift doors were closing. *Shit!* He raced to the stairwell and raced down the four flights of stairs. He made it to the main door just as it was closing behind her. "Abigail!" he shouted. She continued to storm towards her car. He ran out after her. "Abigail. Please."

"Stay away from me, Henry!" she shouted. Tears were welling in her eyes. She fumbled in her bag for her keys. Just as she got the car door open, he arrived beside her.

"Abigail. I'm sorry. Please come back upstairs so we can talk properly."

Just then a passer-by hurried over to Abi's car. "Is everything OK here?" She glared at Henry.

Abi tried hard to keep her composure. "Yes, thank you. I was just leaving."

"Abigail, you know where I am if you need me."

She didn't say a word as she got into the car and started the engine. The woman waited until Abi had driven away before she carried on, giving Henry another suspicious look.

Abi could barely see the road through her tears and had to pull over and stop the car. Unable to keep it in, she let out a long scream and banged her fists on the steering wheel. *How dare Henry say those things? It's obvious that he's just jealous – he wants me and I don't want him. That has to be it. And as for Glenda – her husband doesn't make a fraction of what Kevin does. She's just jealous too. How could I not have seen it before? The only problem in my marriage is me, not Kevin. He's only mean when he hasn't had a good day at work. I'm just being selfish, wanting his attention, when I know he's been busy at work and needs time for himself. And there's no way he's cheating on me. He can't be. My so-called friends have just made up those rumours because they're jealous. In fact, Nikki has probably tried it on with Kevin and he's rejected her. If anything, I'm the one who's been cheating. Sneaking around with Henry behind Kevin's back.*

She fished a tissue from the glove compartment and blew her nose. Kevin wasn't *abusive* – that was all in Henry's head. She could admit that things weren't great in her marriage, but it was her fault. She hadn't made any effort in a long time, but she was going to put that right. She started the car and headed for home, determined to fix her marriage.

***

That night she pulled out all the stops. She made one of Kevin's favourite meals — roast chicken with all the trimmings. She applied fresh make-up, sprayed on some perfume and even put on a flattering dress. Kevin liked it when she wore dresses. She was waiting by the kitchen door when he walked in.

"You look nice," he mumbled, handing her his suit jacket.

Her heart nearly burst. She couldn't remember the last time he had complimented her appearance. It was working. She just had to put in the effort.

"You know, Abs…" he sighed. "You used to make an effort like this every night. You've really let yourself slide."

She tried not to let his comment bother her because he was right; she had let herself slide. She'd do better from now on. That would make him happy.

She poured the wine and sat down at the table opposite him. She thought he looked tired — and no wonder. He worked extremely hard. She couldn't even remember the last time she'd thanked him for all his hard work that enabled their family to enjoy such a good standard of living. Feeling guilty, she gave him a little smile as he took his first bite. "How was your day, honey?" He loved it when she asked him about his day.

He poked at the food on his plate with his fork. "Abs, is this last week's dinner?"

"What do you mean?"

"I mean, the chicken's dry. I'm not sure if these are meant to be potatoes, and I'm going to need the carving knife to slice the gravy."

Ignore him. He doesn't mean it. He's had a hard day.

She took her first bite. But as she chewed, she thought, for once, he's not wrong. The asparagus had turned to mush and the chicken was more than dry; it was incinerated. She took a sip of wine and suddenly realised that this was the first time she had agreed with Kevin about anything in years. But when she took a second sip, it hit her. The dinner *was* awful, but that wasn't her fault. It was Kevin's. He'd said he would be home at six and he liked fifteen minutes to change, so she'd planned dinner to be ready at quarter past six. But he'd been late. She'd expected him at any minute, so she tried to keep it warm. Then at six thirty, when there was still so sign of him, she gave Emma dinner – so at least one member of the family got to enjoy their meal. At eight, when she put Emma to bed he still wasn't home. He hadn't replied to any of her texts or answered her calls, and she'd been worried sick about him. Where was he? Had he been in a car accident on the way home from the train station? He finally turned up at eight thirty, without an excuse or an apology.

And this was far from the first time.

She thought back to the other times he'd criticised her cooking. The eggs were too runny or not runny enough. The tomato soup she'd made from scratch was too tomatoey. Just last week she'd made steak Diane with Lyonnaise potatoes and Kevin had turned his nose up at it because the mushrooms in the sauce were the wrong size. Everyone else she had ever cooked for enjoyed the food she made. Despite his complaints, Kevin nearly always cleared his plate. Was Henry right? Was Kevin being mean? And it wasn't just food. She couldn't remember anything nice he had said to her, or done for her, in years. Yes, he bought her expensive jewellery, but he insisted she wear it every day and made her feel ungrateful when she didn't. And the SUV he'd given her for her thirtieth birthday was completely over the top. When he'd suggested buying it, she told him she wouldn't be comfortable driving something so big and asked for something smaller. But 'something smaller' wouldn't show off Kevin's money, would it? He always wanted people to know how much money he had.

Maybe … maybe there was some truth in what Henry had said. She always did her best and Kevin never appreciated it or thanked her for it. Instead he undermined and ridiculed her at every opportunity. She looked back at some of the major decisions in her life: giving up her job, having a baby, dyeing her hair, getting rid of her books … they had all been his decisions. He always told her she was fat – but she was a size ten and watched what she ate so she could stay that way. He said he didn't find her attractive, but always wanted sex. He'd turned her against most of her friends, and always insisted on knowing where she was.

She tried to fight back tears as realisation flooded over her. *She* wasn't the problem in her marriage, it was Kevin. The reason she could never make him happy was because he wouldn't let her. And, worse than that, he had made her hate herself. Think that she was the problem. Henry was right; she had to do something. *Henry!* What had she done? She'd called him pathetic when he was only trying to be a good friend. She was the pathetic one for letting Kevin treat her the way he did. She was a strong, confident woman — at least, she used to be — and she was going to put a stop to it there and then. Things would change.

She glared at Kevin. He was mumbling something about how she should take cooking lessons. "How about it?"

She felt something inside her snap. "How about … you cook your own dinner from now on?"

His jaw dropped. "What the hell did you just say to me?"

She got up and approached him. She stood up straight and took a deep breath. "I said, *cook your own damn dinner*."

Before he knew what was happening, she had snatched his plate and stormed to the bin. She slammed her foot on the pedal and threw the plate inside. She turned back to him. He was still holding his knife and fork and looking at her in amazement.

"I'm leaving you."

He laughed scornfully and threw his cutlery on the table. "Come on, Abs! There's no need to make such a big deal. I'm just asking you to learn how to cook."

She raised her voice. "And how to dress. What make-up to wear. Who I can and can't have tea with. You're too controlling. I won't take it any more!"

"OK." He sighed. "If you want to leave, there's the fucking door!" Now he was shouting. "Go back to the gutter I dragged you out of. You won't last two minutes without me."

She matched his tone. "I did perfectly fine before we met."

"What? Showing slums to minimum-wage losers for a measly half a per cent? I made more money than you when I was taking a dump. Just go. I've got women lined up around the corner to take your place."

"They're welcome to you. And your bullshit." She marched towards the door.

"Don't let the door hit you on the way out. Oh, and Abs…"

She turned to find him glaring at her.

"Emma stays where she is." He looked her dead in the eye. "There's no way you're taking my daughter out of this house."

Abi froze. She took a deep breath. "I'm not leaving without her."

"Then *you* are not leaving."

He watched her to see her reaction. He couldn't believe she was about to leave him. He'd been through lots of women before he met her – and after – but none that were marriage material. When he met Abi, he knew he had to have her. She was a few years younger than him, beautiful and had a great figure. She was obedient, sensible and didn't have ideas above her station. He knew she would make a good wife and mother – although her pregnancy and age had taken their toll on her body, and he knew he would replace her one day with a younger, firmer model. But that would be on his terms, and definitely when Emma was old enough not to need waited on hand and foot. He sighed. He had a deal to close.

He lowered his head and looked up at her with his best sincere impression. "Abs, I am so sorry. I know I've been a bit snappy with you recently, but it's just because I'm under so much pressure at work. You know I have to suck up to people all the time. It's exhausting. When I come home, I just need to blow off a bit of steam, and I guess I let it out on you. But I thought you were in on the joke."

"It's a joke?" she asked quietly.

He smiled. "Yes, of course it's a joke. Look at you – you're perfect. You're beautiful and sexy. I didn't know that the things I said actually upset you, or I would never have said them. Now that I know, I'll stop. I promise. I love you and I love our daughter and the beautiful home you've made us here."

"You think I'm beautiful and sexy? But you always call me Fat Abs."

He sank his head in his hands. "Oh, Abs! I meant it ironically, because you're so beautiful. It's a term of endearment. I'm so sorry, I had no idea you thought it was insulting. I'm so sorry, you know I really fancy you." He bit the inside of his cheek. "And I was only kidding about the other women. I flirt sometimes, but that's as far as it goes. I promise."

"But what about the nights you don't come home?"

"I've told you loads of times. Whenever I miss the last train home, Robert lets me crash on his sofa and his missus throws me out first thing in the morning. She's not an amazing wife like you. No full English."

"Even though I never get the eggs right?"

He sighed. "I'm so sorry. I'm a terrible husband. I don't deserve you. My friends are all so jealous of me, having you. I'm sorry if you think I've been taking you for granted."

She sighed. Perhaps she had been taking him for granted too. Especially when she'd been seeing Henry. But now she could see Henry for what he was. He was lying, twisting things, to make her leave Kevin. He was trying to manipulate her.

Kevin tried to figure out what was going on in her head.

He could see that his pitch was working and she was relenting. He knew he didn't have to do much more to close the deal. Maybe if he added a little incentive... He got down on his knees and took her gently by the hand.

"Come on, give me another chance. I'm begging you. I'll do anything you want."

She nodded. "Anything?"

"Anything."

"Don't go out drinking on Friday night or on Saturday after football."

He winced. "Is this about the jeans and Emma's cake?"

"Yes."

"I'm so sorry. I was drunk and I didn't know what I was doing."

"And you're too critical of me. Telling me to wear more make-up, how to dress and what I cook is never good enough..."

"I'm sorry. You always look stunning and you're an amazing chef. But I also know that you like everything to be perfect, so when I see something not quite perfect, I point it out to you so you can put it right. I thought I was helping you."

"Helping? By destroying my beautiful cake?"

"I just thought if you had bought a cake, like I told you to, you wouldn't have had as much work to do."

"Stop telling me what to do!" she yelled. "And don't tell me where I can and can't go. You're too controlling."

"It's not controlling! I'm only trying to protect you. It's my job as your husband."

"I don't need that sort of protection. What I need is a husband who lets me be myself, and I'm thirty years old – I can make my own decisions."

"Oh, Abs, you're an incredible woman to put up with an idiot like me. I'm so sorry. Please don't leave me, I don't know what I'd do without you. I swear to you I'll try and be a better husband. I'll stop the silly jokes and I'll definitely go easy on the booze. How about I see if that old biddy next door will watch Emma, like she's always offering to do, and I'll take you out to dinner tomorrow night. Like we used to."

"I'd really like that."

"Good. Me too. It's been ages since we spent proper time together."

She smiled and pulled him up from the floor. He locked eyes with her and sighed. "I haven't seen that smile in a long time. I hope that means that I'm forgiven?"

She nodded.

"Good. Thank you. You know, you're really sexy when you're angry." He raised his eyebrows. "That fight got me all worked up. How about we go upstairs and make up properly?"

She glared at him.

He held up his hands. "OK. You're still cross with me, and you're right to be. Why don't you go and read a magazine or take a bath? I'll fish my dinner out of the bin."

"You don't have to eat that. I'll make you something else."

"No." He pointed at her. "I'm going to eat the dinner my beautiful wife made for me. Right out of the bin, like the dog that I am."

She laughed to herself as she left the kitchen. She was so relieved. She couldn't believe that Henry had nearly talked her into leaving when all she'd had to do was to talk to Kevin. It had actually gone better than she could have hoped. She felt reassured as she went up to the bathroom. Everything was going to be OK. He did love her and had promised to try to be a better husband, and she would try to be a better wife. And he was already living up to his promise. It was so nice of him to suggest she took a bath instead of making him more food. She decided she would put on some nice lingerie after her bath. Just in case he still wanted sex. After all, he was making an effort; she should too.

Chapter Fifteen

For the next few weeks, Kevin was the perfect husband. He was drinking less, and he was kind and attentive. Every night he came home promptly after work and always brought something home for Abi: flowers, magazines, chocolates. Once he brought her a new iron and enquired whether she needed a new vacuum cleaner too. They went out for dinner at least twice a week and he even picked up on her hints and took her to see *Hamilton* in the West End. She was falling in love with Kevin again and couldn't remember ever being so happy. There was only one thing wrong. Emma was unhappy. She missed Toby and asked about him every Saturday – and Henry too. Abi felt guilty about the horrible things she had said to him when he'd only been trying to help. If it hadn't had been for him, she would never have talked to Kevin and nothing would have changed.

She had to talk to Henry and make things right. Maybe they could be friends again.

***

Abi was nervous when she arrived at the soft play centre. She wasn't even sure if Henry would be there. But as soon as they walked into the play area, Emma spotted Toby and ran straight to him. Abi was amazed that they ran off together as usual without any questions about the missing weeks. They were just happy to see each other.

It took a moment for Abi to spot Henry because he wasn't sitting at *their* table. He was at a table in the corner, his nose in a book. She walked over to him and stood behind a free seat. "Do you mind if I sit here?"

He looked up from his book and smiled. Quickly, he closed the book and got up to pull the chair out for her. He gave her shoulder a gentle squeeze before he sat back down. They sat in silence.

Henry had never seen her look so beautiful, or so relaxed. Not that he'd dare mention it, but she had put on a few pounds and looked all the better for it. "I almost didn't recognise you. You look great as a brunette. How come you dyed your hair?"

She tucked a loose strand behind her ear. "Henry, you must have known I wasn't a natural blonde. My colourist is good, but not that good. This is as close to my natural colour as she could get, but it'll grow in."

"Honestly, I had no idea. You look great."

"Thank you. You look good too." She cleared her throat and looked around the room. "I wasn't sure if you still came here."

"I've come every week … hoping to run into you. I didn't like how we left things. I was worried about you, but I knew you wouldn't want me to call or come to your house. I knew you'd come here if you wanted to talk to me."

"I'm so sorry about the other week—"

He held up his hand to stop her, but she persisted.

"I said some really awful things to you. I know you were just trying to be a good friend to me, but I think you got the wrong end of the stick. Yes, Kevin and I were going through a bad patch, but we've talked and he's apologised. He's been a different man these past few weeks, really kind and attentive. Things are almost back to the way they were when we were first married. We're having date nights, we've been to the theatre, and he even made me breakfast in bed."

It had been a piece of burned toast and a lukewarm cup of tea, but she thought it was a step in the right direction.

"I'm happy for you, Abigail. And he must be doing something right because I've never seen you look so beautiful."

"Thank you."

"I'd really like it if we could still be friends. If you're allowed, that is?"

She gave him a reproachful look. "Of course I'm allowed to have friends, and I'd like that too. But just this – things with the kids – nothing behind closed doors. It wouldn't be fair to Kevin."

"Or to Colette."

"Colette?" Abi shifted in her seat.

"She works with Becca at the surgery. Apparently, she's fancied me for years and she's been dropping hints at Becca to set us up. We've texted and talked on the phone a few times. We have our first date tonight. She's a GP. She's pretty, funny and I don't think she's ever even said the word 'appropriate'."

Abi laughed. "She sounds perfect for you. I'm glad you've met someone."

"Thanks." He was already feeling guilty about Colette, but it was phase one of his plan to move on with his life. "It's just dinner."

"You don't have to explain yourself to me. I'm glad you're happy."

"I'm trying. You're not going to be easy to get over."

"I'm sorry, Henry. Things could have been

129

different, but I have to give my marriage another chance. For Emma's sake."

"I know." He nodded. "I just want you to be happy."

"I want that for you too." She searched the play frame for Emma. "I should go."

"But you've just got here. I'm sure the kids will want to spend some time together. Please stay for a cup of tea. It's my round."

She glanced over at Emma and Toby, who were doing laps of the obstacle course. Emma really looked like she was enjoying herself. Abi thought it would be a shame to drag her away. "OK. But just one cup."

They gave each other reassuring smiles and tried to work out how to be comfortable together again. "So, what have I missed in here the past few weeks?" Abi offered as a safe conversation starter.

Henry rolled his eyes. "Where do I start? I'll get the tea and scone and fill you in."

She stopped him as he stood up. "Actually, I'll have a muffin. Double chocolate."

"Do I still get half?"

She smiled and shook her head. "Get your own."

***

That evening Abi and Kevin were canoodling over the dessert menu in their favourite Italian restaurant. He stroked the back of her hand. "What are you going to have?"

"Hmm, I can't decide. I used to always get the cheesecake, but I like the sound of the crème brûlée."

"Remember what we used to do? You get the cheesecake and I'll get the crème brûlée and we'll swap halfway through."

"Sounds good," she cooed, "unless I don't like the crème brûlée, in which case we swap straight back."

"It's the woman's prerogative – and you're a very beautiful woman."

"Don't." She fluttered her eyelashes.

"I mean it. You're the best-looking woman in here by miles." He looked around the restaurant to check no one was watching, then began to play with her foot under the table.

"You actually scrub up well too. Is that a new shirt?"

He puffed out his chest. "Yes, I bought it myself. Do you like it? It's not as nice as the ones you usually pick for me, but I thought it would do."

"Oh, it does," she teased as she ran her foot up his leg.

"Are you flirting with me, Mrs Preston?"

"Yes, Mr Preston."

He was looking at her with his best 'come to bed' expression when they were interrupted by Abi's friend Nikki.

"Hey guys, I haven't seen you two here in forever. How are you?"

"We're good, Nikki, thanks." Abi smiled at Kevin, happy that, for once, she didn't have to pretend. She really did feel good – about herself and her marriage.

"You're looking well, Kevin," Nikki purred.

Kevin smiled and nodded politely, not looking remotely interested in anything Nikki had to say.

Abi rolled her eyes. "It's lovely to see you, but you're kind of interrupting date night." She gestured as subtly as she could for Nikki to make herself scarce.

Finally taking the hint, Nikki made her excuses. "I

get it. Sorry, guys, I'll leave you to it." She was about to walk away when she turned back to Abi. "Oh hey, I know who I'd love to date. That friend of yours. What's his name?"

Kevin suddenly looked interested.

Abi shifted in her seat. "I'm not sure who you're talking about. I'll give you a call tomorrow and we'll chat."

"You know exactly who I mean. That hot English teacher who just got divorced. He was at Emma's birthday party with his kid – and I've heard that you've been practically joined at the hip with him at soft play."

Abi gave a nervous laugh. "Just let me phone you tomorrow."

Nikki glanced at Kevin, whose face was turning red. She gave Abi an apologetic shrug. "Of course. Speak to you tomorrow." She mouthed 'sorry' and scurried off.

Abi looked at Kevin, whose face was now bright red. Just as she opened her mouth to speak, the waiter arrived to take their order. "Who's for dessert?"

Kevin cracked his knuckles under the table but forced a smile for the waiter. "Actually, we can't stay. We've just had a call from the babysitter – there's an emergency at home. Just bring us each a shot of Jack Daniels when you bring the bill. And can you please call us a taxi to Richmond Hill."

"Certainly, sir."

"On second thoughts, make those drinks doubles."

The waiter winked. "I like your style."

Abi's eyes darted to the second empty wine bottle on their table. She'd only had two glasses, meaning Kevin had had quite a bit to drink already. She waited

132

for the waiter to leave before she spoke. "Kevin, I know what you're probably thinking. But there's a really innocent explanation."

He placed his elbows on the table and rested his chin on his clenched fists. "Is there, Abs? Because you look guilty as hell."

"He's just a dad from school."

He nodded. "OK. If he's just a dad from school, how come Nikki doesn't know him? That slut knows all the dads."

She cleared her throat. "Did I say school? I meant soft play."

"Are you having some trouble getting your story straight? Would you like me to give you a few minutes?"

"No. There's no trouble. And there's no story. He's Toby's dad. Emma's always talking about Toby."

"Toby's dad? Hmm, that's funny, because you've only mentioned Toby's mum and Nikki says he's divorced." He scratched his head. "So, you see him at that soft play place every week? And what do you do after that?"

"Nothing. I usually collect your dry cleaning and go to Sainsbury's. Then I go home."

"Whose home? Mine, or his?"

"Ours," she said firmly.

He snorted. "Would that be the home you threatened to walk out of a couple of weeks ago? You were going to run off with him. Weren't you?"

"No. I was going to go to my sister's."

"Jesus, I'd like to see that! She's more of a mess than you."

"Don't say that about my sister."

He pointed his finger at her. "Don't you dare talk

back to me, Abs. You're meant to be grovelling."

"I won't grovel, because I've done nothing wrong."

"I'll be the judge of that." He forced another smile as the waiter brought the drinks and the bill.

"Your taxi will be outside in a moment."

Abi reached for her glass, but Kevin snatched it from her. "That's not for you." He put the glass to his mouth and swallowed the Jack Daniels in one gulp. Then he took his own glass and did the same. He took out his wallet and threw a few twenties onto the table, then stood up and picked up Abi's coat and bag. "Let's get you home, Abs."

She trembled as he put his arm around her waist and escorted her to the taxi.

They were silent on the journey home. Kevin sat in the passenger seat and stared out of the window, rage building inside him. *My wife, fooling around with another man while I'm at football on Saturdays? And she's probably sleeping with him during the week too, when I'm at work. If Nikki knows, the whole town must know. They've probably all been talking about me behind my back. That little bitch is making me a laughing stock. She'll regret it.* He clenched his fists. *She needs to be reminded who's in charge.*

Abi sat alone in the back seat and replayed their conversation in her head, trying to prepare answers for the questions she thought Kevin might ask. She tried to convince herself that Kevin was a reasonable man, that he would understand that she had done nothing wrong. But deep down she knew he was irrational and jealous. He hated it if another man so much as looked at her. He often accused her of leading them on. That's why she'd started to dress more conservatively for her age – to stop men looking at her. It wasn't her decision, but neither were most of her decisions. Kevin was controlling her, and she hadn't even noticed.

If Henry was right about that, could he be right about Kevin physically hurting me? I know he gets into fights, because he's come home with a black eye or bloodied nose before, but he told me he'd been hurt at football. I had no reason to suspect he wasn't telling the truth. But could he be violent towards me? She touched the small scar on her temple.

They hadn't been married long when she got it. One afternoon she had returned home from a shopping trip to find Kevin sitting at the kitchen table, drinking.

"Hi, honey. You're home early."

"Very sorry to inconvenience you," he snapped, then pointed to her short skirt and heels. "Did you have something else planned?"

"Oh, I just meant … I wasn't expecting you until six."

"Well, I'm here now. And remember, I can come home at any time." He gestured to the bags. "Looks like you've been busy. Any sexy lingerie in there?"

"Maybe," she teased, but it had been the sole reason for her shopping trip. He'd been dropping heavy hints that her underwear wasn't alluring enough.

"Good girl. You can model it for me after dinner." He poured another drink. "And what is for dinner? I'm starving."

"Um, I'm not sure yet. There's plenty to choose from in the fridge: chicken breast, mince, salmon. Why don't you have a look and take out what you fancy, and I'll start it right after I pop these upstairs." She kissed him on the cheek. He glared at her as she hurried out of the kitchen with the bags.

In their bedroom, she was about to throw the bags onto the bed when she remembered: the last time she did that, Kevin had thrown her 'mess' into the bin. She tucked the bags neatly in her wardrobe, then kicked off her shoes and sat down on the bed. She reached for her pyjama bottoms, then stopped. The last time she had changed so early in the day, Kevin had asked what time her friends were arriving for their sleepover. He preferred Abi to keep a more formal appearance, at least until after dinner. So she slipped her heels back on and went downstairs.

Kevin was rooting through his drinks cupboard when she came up behind him and placed her hand on his shoulder.

"Did you pick someth—"

The cupboard door slammed against her face. She cried out in pain, stumbled backwards, and put her hand to her temple. She felt the warm trickle of blood from her nose, then saw it drip onto the floor.

"Abs! Why on earth did you creep up behind me?"

"I wasn't creeping," she sobbed as she struggled to a chair.

Kevin glared at her "I didn't know you were there. You better not think I did that on purpose!"

She shook her head, trembling.

"Good girl." He got some kitchen roll, which he held under the cold tap for a few seconds before offering it to her for her nose. He got another piece and dabbed the blood away from her temple. "The handle has barely broken your skin."

"Do you think I'll need stitches?"

"No!" he snapped. "It's just a scratch. It probably won't even leave a scar."

But it did leave a scar, and not just a physical one. Even though Kevin eventually apologised and made a fuss of her for the next few days, for some reason, she didn't entirely believe it had been an accident.

When the taxi slowed down and turned off the main road onto Richmond Hill, Abi had a dreadful feeling that there was about to be another *accident*.

As soon as they got into the house, Kevin ushered Abi into the living room. Mrs Smith, their neighbour, looked at the clock. "You're home early. Is everything all right?"

"Abs felt a bit poorly, so we thought it was best to come home."

Abi stood in silence as Mrs Smith examined her. "You do look pale, dear. Would you like me to make you some hot, sweet tea before I go?"

"That would be lovely. Thank you," Abi said quickly.

Mrs Smith nodded and left the living room to go to the kitchen. Abi tried to follow but Kevin grabbed her by the arm. She froze. He'd never done anything like that to her before.

"Don't make things worse for yourself. Sit down. I'll deal with you in a minute." He pushed her down onto the sofa. "Oh, Mrs Smith…"

He left the living room and closed the door behind him.

Abi sat up straight on the sofa and tried to listen to their muffled voices. After a few minutes she heard the front door open, then close. Then the living room door opened. She looked up to see Kevin standing in the doorway: all six foot two and fifteen stone of him. He held what looked like a full glass of whisky.

Never before had she seen the look that was on

his face. He was so angry. "You've been making a fool out of me," he said slowly.

"No, I haven't. It's not what you think. We're just friends, he's just—"

"I know. He's just a friend." He stepped into the room. "A friend you kept secret. A friend you see behind my back. A friend you were talking to at Emma's party, and when I asked you who he was you pretended you didn't know him." He closed the door and leaned against it. "You must think I'm stupid."

"No." Her voice trembled. "I don't."

He drained the glass, then took a step towards her. He slammed the glass down on the coffee table beside the sofa. "I think you do. Otherwise you wouldn't dare to sneak around behind my back while I'm hard at work. And this is how you repay me – by having an affair?"

"I'm not having an affair." Her voice was quiet.

He took another step towards the sofa. "Of course you are. It's obvious now. You've been different these past few months. You're talking back to me, cutting up my clothes, changing your hair. You even threatened to leave me. Now I know why. You're planning to run off with him."

"No, Kevin. I wanted to leave because you weren't being nice to me."

"Not nice to you?" He laughed. "Abs, if I had a hissy fit every time someone wasn't nice to me, do you think I'd be where I am now? Suck it up! You're sitting pretty here. I can't believe the way you've behaved. And after all I've done for you the past few weeks. I've bent over backwards trying to make you feel special."

"You shouldn't have to bend over backwards. Or try to make me feel special. And the last few weeks don't make up for the years you've made me feel like nothing. You made me hate myself, but all the time it was you I should have been hating." She tried to stand up, but he placed his hands firmly on her shoulders and forced her back down on the sofa.

"You ungrateful little bitch." He leaned down to her and pointed his finger right in her face. "You have the nicest clothes, nicest car and nicest house of anyone you know. I've given you those things and I can take them away. You've been free to come and go as you please and spend whatever you like, but only because I let you. All of that stops right now. You have to earn my trust again. Hand over your credit cards and your mobile phone. From now on, you'll only leave this house to take Emma to school and back. And you don't go anywhere or see anyone unless you get my permission first."

She looked him in the eye. "No."

He growled at her, "I wasn't asking."

She stood up and tried to push past him. He grabbed her arm again, digging his fingernails into her wrist. A sharp pain shot up her arm as he twisted it. "Kevin, let go. You're hurting me!"

He twisted it further. "I'm hurting you? You're the one who's having an affair."

"I'm not." She tried to pull away from him, but he held her wrist tightly. "But I know you are. I've heard about you and your women."

He let go of her wrist and raised his hand to hit her, but she pulled away and looked back at him in disgust. "I'm taking Emma and we're leaving right now." She pushed past him towards the door.

As she reached for the handle, he hissed, "Take one more step, Abigail, and I swear to God I'll make you regret it."

She froze. *This is it. This is what Henry meant. How could I have been so stupid? I should have listened to him. I have to get out of here.* She grabbed the handle. Just as she was pulling the door open, he came up behind her, reached over her shoulder and pushed the door closed. She tried her hardest to pull it open, but he was taller and stronger than her.

She couldn't stop the tears that rolled down her cheeks as she realised what was about to happen. There was nothing she could do. She could scream, but the only one to hear would be Emma, and Abi couldn't risk her coming downstairs. Maybe he would go easier on her if she didn't put up a fight. Slowly, she turned to face him.

His eyes widened at the sight of her tears and he let out a sigh. "Oh, Abs..."

She flinched as he put his hand out to touch her cheek but, much to her surprise, he gently wiped away her tears. She let out the breath she had been holding. Relief flooded over her. He wasn't going to hurt her. He loved her, and everything was going to be OK. "I'm sorry," she whispered. Then she bowed her head and rested it on his chest.

He wrapped his arms around her and kissed the top of her head. "I know." He looked deep into her eyes as he pushed her up against the door. "And this is the last thing I want to do. But you've been letting yourself slip for years and now ... now you've disrespected me. I have to teach you a lesson so it never happens again."

She stood, paralysed with fear. There was nothing she could do.

"You'll thank me for it one day."

***

Henry asked for the bill while Colette was in the ladies' room. Overall, their first date hadn't been that bad. She was beautiful, smart and funny. He had genuinely enjoyed himself, even though Abi was constantly in the back of his mind. He wondered how her date night was going with Kevin. That morning at the soft play centre she had looked so beautiful. She was obviously happy with Kevin and their marriage was solid. That's why he had lied about having a date with Colette – to save face, show he had moved on. He had spoken to Colette a few times but it wasn't until after he'd seen how happy Abi was that he knew he had to start dating again. He had to let her go, once and for all. So he called Colette. Luckily, she had no plans for that evening.

He was keying his PIN into the card machine when she returned from the ladies' room.

"Henry! We agreed to go Dutch." She smiled.

The waiter nodded apologetically and left them to it.

"I'm sorry. I can't let a lady pay for dinner. Well, not one as pretty as you."

She blushed as she sat back down at the table. "Becca warned me about your charm."

"It's not charm. It's honesty."

"There you go again."

He held his hands up. "Sorry. I'll stop being charming if that's what you want."

"No, keep going." She took the last sip of her wine. "I was actually a bit nervous about tonight. I didn't date much when I was younger – I was always too busy studying. And at uni when all my friends were dating, I was working to help pay my fees. I thought there'd be time for dating later. Then, after seven years at uni, I realised that all the good men were taken. All that was left were chauvinist playboys and divorced guys. No offence, but I didn't really want to date anyone who was divorced because they usually have so much baggage. And there must be something wrong with them, I thought, otherwise why would they be divorced?"

"Ouch." He pretended to be offended.

"Present company excluded."

"Thanks. And I don't mean to sound rude, but I don't think of my son as baggage. We're more of a package deal. He's the most important thing in my life."

She clapped her hand to her mouth. "I'm so sorry. That's not what I meant. I've just had some friends go out with divorced men, and their ex-wives seem fond of causing trouble. I know that's not the case with Becca. I still can't believe she set us up. If your ex-wife doesn't have a bad word to say about you, then you must be OK."

"'You must be OK'. I think that's the nicest thing anyone's ever said about me. But I'm sure, if you pressed her, Becca would be able to come up with something."

They laughed and she looked at her watch. "It's still early. Do you want to go somewhere else for a drink?"

Actually, he did. He knew that Steve and some of their mutual friends were out having a drink at the Red Lion. They could 'accidentally' run into them, take the pressure off the date a bit. "Sure. Do you want to go to the Red Lion?"

"I was actually thinking about … my place." She raised an eyebrow.

Her place? He was taken aback. She was lovely, and he did want to get to know her, so another date wouldn't be out of the question. But go back to her place? The look in her eye gave him the impression that there was a good chance she wanted more than a drink. He wasn't sure. He hadn't resolved his feelings for Abi and didn't want to use Colette as a rebound. But how else would he get over Abi if he didn't date? And how could he—

"You can just say no, Henry." Colette picked up her handbag.

He cleared his throat. "I'm sorry. I'm still working things out about my divorce, so I don't want to rush into anything. Yes. Let's go back to your place for a drink. But just a drink, for now."

She blushed.

He noticed. "I'm sorry. I've either been too presumptuous or I've offended you. Either way I've ruined this. Haven't I?"

"No, Henry." She laughed. "Come on, let's have a drink. I promise I won't take advantage of you."

He relaxed and gave a cheeky grin. "OK. But I'll let you know when you can take advantage of me."

"I can't wait." She smirked. "Let's get out of here."

In the taxi on the way home, Colette snuggled close to Henry. He tried to keep his gaze straight ahead, but out of the corner of his eye he could see that her dress had crept up her thigh when she had crossed her legs. Her chest was pressed against his arm and a quick glance confirmed what he had suspected in the restaurant — she wasn't wearing a bra. This, combined with the aroma of her recently reapplied perfume, should have been enough to get Henry excited about going home with her. But he felt nothing. He was confused. Why wasn't he interested in this beautiful woman who was practically sitting on top of him, offering herself to him? All he felt was guilt. As if he was cheating on Abi somehow.

Then it finally dawned on him. He was in love with Abi. He'd suspected it many times, but had tried to shrug it off as friendship, lust, even loneliness. But now, faced with the prospect of being with a woman other than Abi, he knew it was love. Even though he'd tried to convince himself that he could let her go, he couldn't. But he had to. She had admitted that she had feelings for him, but that wasn't enough – *he* wasn't enough. Kevin could give her everything she wanted, and he was her daughter's father. There was no way he could compete.

The taxi slowed as it pulled into a cul-de-sac and Colette said to the driver, "Just here on the left. After the lamppost."

The taxi stopped. Henry jumped out and offered her his hand. She gave him a coy smile as he helped her out of the car. He thought she looked really pretty, but she also looked vulnerable. And hopeful. He couldn't lead her on. He took her other hand in his. "I'm so sorry, Colette. I can't come in."

She took a step backwards.

He didn't even try to make up an excuse; he owed her that. "I'm in love with someone else."

"Henry. Becca has moved on," she said quietly.

"It's not Becca. Goodnight, Colette." He raised her hand to his mouth and kissed it. "I'm sorry."

"I'm sorry too." She pulled her hand from his and without another word turned her back on him. She opened the small gate and walked up the path to her front door.

Henry got into the passenger seat beside the driver, and asked him to wait until Colette had unlocked the door and gone inside.

"Where to?" the driver asked.

"Richmond Hill." The words were out of his mouth before he knew what he was saying.

"Oh, nice."

Yeah. It really would be. "Scratch that. Can you take me back to town? The Red Lion."

"To try again? She seemed up for it. What was the matter with her?"

"Nothing. She's just not the one."

"Oh. Does 'the one' live in Richmond Hill?"

He nodded. "But she's made her choice."

"Town it is, then. To drown your sorrows."

"Thanks." He took out his mobile and selected Abi's number. He stared at the green button the whole way back to town.

When he arrived at the pub, he found Steve at a table with a group of friends. He groaned when he saw Becca was there too. She was glaring at him. He pulled a chair from a nearby table and joined them.

"I just had a text from Colette. She said you were hot and cold all night and then you just blew her off. I can't believe you."

Steve recognised her tone and jumped up. "I'll get the condemned man a pint." He clapped Henry on the shoulder and hurried off to the bar.

"I'm sorry about Colette."

"No. I won't accept sorry. I assume it's Abi you're in love with. What the hell is wrong with you? She's married. Forget about her!"

145

But he couldn't forget about her. He was in love with her. "Can you please stop? I don't want to talk about it. I just want a couple of drinks with my friends. Please don't be my ex-wife right now. And by the way, if we're both here, who's looking after Toby?"

"Babysitter. And don't try to change the subject. You're just cross with me because I'm right."

"She's always right. You should know that better than me," Steve said, placing a pint in front of Henry and sitting down. "Hey, Bec, that asshole we had the run-in with a few weeks ago has just arrived."

"Uh! He makes my skin crawl." She shuddered.

Henry grimaced and looked behind him. "Which one?"

Becca pointed to a man at the bar who was trying to chat up a group of women.

Henry's jaw dropped, "Oh my God. That's Kevin Preston!"

"Who the hell is Kevin Preston?"

"Abigail's husband."

Becca's eyes widened. She looked behind her and then back at Henry. "*That* is Abi's husband? Please tell me you're joking. He's a horrible man."

"I wish I was." His blood was starting to boil. He glared at Kevin, who was ordering a round of drinks for the women. They were all laughing and giggling with him. What the hell did he think he was doing?

"No. She can't be married to him. She's lovely, and so sweet. He's a complete and utter asshole. He grabbed my bum a few weeks ago and when I slapped his hand away, he threatened to hit me back."

"He did what?"

"Threatened to hit me. Steve saw the commotion and came over to see what was going on, and the asshole took a swipe at him. Luckily, he was blind drunk, so he missed and hit the deck. Barman threw him out."

Henry looked at Steve for confirmation. Steve nodded. Then Becca's eyes widened. "Remember I told you how Emma behaved at the zoo? Now I know which parent she learned that from." She bit her fingernail. "He threatened to hit me. He took a swipe at Steve. You don't think he…"

Steve tried to reassure her. "It could be all talk. The guy was drunk. It was probably a one-off."

"But we've seen him in here loads. And, now that I think of it, he's always with a different woman."

Henry's head was spinning. A huge anger was building up inside him. His suspicions of Kevin had been right. He still couldn't be sure about abuse, but Kevin was almost certainly guilty of being unfaithful. "He can't treat Abigail like that. I'm going over there." He pushed his chair back and was about to stand up when Steve pulled him back down.

"Mate. Leave it. You'll only end up in a brawl. Just try to forget about him and enjoy your pint."

Henry looked at him as if he was insane. "Are you kidding? You expect me to forget about it? We're all here having a nice quiet drink. He's here either threatening women or trying to shag every woman he sees. All the while, poor Abi is sitting at home alone thinking her husband is a saint. I saw her just this morning. She looked so happy. She has no idea what kind of man she's married to."

Becca sighed. "If she looked happy, she probably is. Maybe he's just acting the big man in here, maybe he is nice at home. Otherwise why would she be with him?"

Henry knew that women stayed in bad or abusive

relationships for many reasons: fear, confusion, embarrassment, even denial. Abuse wasn't always as obvious as physical violence; it could be so subtle that it was never seen. When they'd argued at his flat a few weeks before, he knew he'd hit a nerve with Abi, and that had been before what he knew now. She'd said she'd talked to Kevin and he was sorry for his behaviour, yet here he was in the pub pawing other women when they were meant to be having a date night. Something wasn't right. He knew it. He knew he had to confront her and tell her how he felt. Maybe he could get her to see who Kevin really was. Now was the time. It didn't look like Kevin was headed home anytime soon, and it might be a long time before he had another opportunity to talk to Abi alone. He raised his pint and took a few mouthfuls for Dutch courage.

"I'm going over to her house now, to talk to her. You guys keep your eyes on Kevin. Ring me if he leaves the bar." He jumped up from the table.

"Henry, you'll only make things worse. Sit down. Now!"

But by the time Becca had finished her sentence, he was gone. She whacked Steve on the arm. "Go after him!"

"No, Becca. Let him go. He's been hung up on her for months, let him get it out of his system. Best case, she listens to him and he gets the girl. Worst case, she sends him packing and he gets some sort of closure from it. Let's just keep an eye on that asshole. Give Henry some time."

"This is a mistake."

"Maybe. But it's Henry's mistake to make. Let him go. He's not your husband any more."

Becca tutted and took a sip of her drink. She

fished her mobile from her bag, set it on the table in front of her and fixed her eyes on Kevin.

***

The taxi dropped Henry off outside Abi's house. He looked around to see if there was anyone watching then hurried up the driveway to the front door. It was probably too late to ring the bell – Emma would be asleep. He took out his mobile and selected Abi's number. It rang until the answer phone clicked on. Maybe she was in bed already? He peered through the side window. There was a light coming from under the kitchen door. He knocked on the door lightly. No answer. He knocked harder. Still no answer. He looked around to make sure there was no one watching and tried the handle. It didn't open. *Sod it, I'll just ring the doorbell. If Emma is anything like Toby, she'll sleep through an avalanche.* He rang the bell. After the third ring, the kitchen door opened slightly, but she didn't come out. He bent down to the letterbox and stuck his hand through it.

"Abigail. It's me, Henry. Please open the door. I need to talk to you. It's really important."

Abi rushed out of the kitchen and across the hall. He stood and waited but the door didn't open. "Abigail?" His heart was pounding. He knocked again.

Shaking, she stood with her back against the door. *Why is he here? He can't see me like this. And what will Kevin do if he comes home to find Henry on his doorstep? I have to make him leave. For everyone's sake.*

"You can't be here," she said through the door.

"It's all right, Abigail. I know Kevin isn't at home –

149

I just saw him at the pub. I've people watching him, and they'll call me when he leaves. I promise I'll be gone before he gets back. He won't know I was here. Just open the door. Give me five minutes. I really need to talk to you."

She was so frighten*ed. If I open the door, Henry will see what Kevin has done and he won't leave. There will be trouble. But what if Henry isn't here when Kevin gets home? What if he's still angry? What if he starts on me again? Henry could help me.* She almost couldn't bear to make the decision. Terrified, she reached for the key and turned it.

He heard the lock click but the door didn't open. He tried the handle and pushed the door open. The hall was still dark but, when he stepped inside, he could see that Abi's whole body was shaking. "Abigail, are you OK?" he whispered.

She didn't answer. He stepped closer but she took a step backwards.

"Abigail? What's wrong?" He held his hand out to her. She was backing away again when she stepped into the stream of light coming from the kitchen. It caught her face. Henry stopped in his tracks. He felt an enormous pressure on his chest and couldn't catch his breath. He felt physically sick and his knees buckled, but he steadied himself. He took a second look at her. She was trembling. Her right eye was swollen and bleeding. Blood had trickled down her face and dripped onto her dress. She just stood there in front of him, expressionless, clutching her wrist. Her eyes were vacant, as if she was staring straight through him.

Henry's first instinct was to run out of the door and straight to the Red Lion. He wanted to see how brave Kevin was up against someone his own size. But he quickly regained his composure. Kevin could wait; Abi was his priority. He needed to comfort her, but he was afraid to touch her. "Abigail. It's going to be OK."

She began to sob.

Very slowly and gently, he approached. She collapsed against him. He held her as she cried and tried his best to hold back his own tears. He couldn't believe what was happening. They stood in the dark hall for a few minutes before he led her back to the kitchen and helped her to a chair. He went to the freezer and searched for the ice cube tray. He grabbed a tea towel from the counter, then spread it out and tipped the ice into it. His mind was in overdrive. How could Kevin have done this? Was it the first time? If not, how many times had he hit her? How long had it been going on?

He returned to Abi, who flinched as his hand approached her face. She took the makeshift ice pack and held it against her eye. It was only then that Henry noticed the bruising on her neck. "What did he do to you, Abigail?"

"He—" She broke down again.

"I'm sorry. It's OK. It's all going to be OK. I'm not going to let him hurt you again, I promise." He knelt down beside her and held his arms out to her. She leaned into him and rested her head on his shoulder. He stroked her hair while she cried. "Have you called the police?"

"No."

He let go of her to take his mobile phone from his pocket. He keyed 999 and set it on the table in front of her.

She stared at it. "I can't."

"You have to."

She shook her head at him.

"Then just give me the nod and I'll do it for you. A few weeks ago, you said this would never happen and now here we are. What if he does it again? What if it's Emma next?"

She began to cry again. "This is all my fault. I should have listened to you."

"No, Abigail," he whispered. "This is not *your* fault. This is Kevin's fault and he's going to go away for a long time for this. He won't be able to hurt you any more."

She stared at the phone. "What do I say?"

"Say your husband assaulted you. They'll know what to do."

She took a deep breath, then picked up the phone.

The female police officer closed her notebook and gave Abi a reassuring smile. "That's all we need for now. I'll get an official statement from you tomorrow, but right now I want to get you to the hospital to get you checked over. Your eye looks like it might need stitches."

She shook her head. "No. My daughter is in bed asleep. I'm not going anywhere while Kevin is still out there."

"We've sent officers down to the pub to look for him—"

"The pub! I can't believe he did this to her and just went to the pub!" Henry clenched his fists.

The officer sighed. "And I'll keep two officers here in case we miss him and he comes back."

"It's all right, dear," said Mrs Smith, her neighbour. She had arrived when she saw the flashing lights. "I'll stay here with Emma. You two go." She broke into tears. "I'm so sorry, dear! I had no idea."

"I did. I should have done something," Henry said as he paced the kitchen. "Wait until I get my hands on him. I'll kill him!"

The police officer gave him a stern look. "Sir, I've told you already, comments like that do not help. One more and I'll ask you to leave."

"No," Abi begged. "He'll be quiet. Won't you, Henry?"

He gave her a frustrated look. He'd just opened his mouth to speak when he felt his mobile buzz in his pocket. He reached for it and saw that it was Becca calling. The kitchen door opened, and they all turned to see another police officer enter. He gave a nod to the female officer, who turned to Abi. "We have your husband in custody. Let me take you to the hospital."

***

Henry waited in the relatives area while Abi was checked over by the doctor. He paced the floor, racked with guilt, feeling helpless and ashamed. Why did he let this happen to Abi? He had known Kevin could be capable of this yet he'd done nothing. He really wanted to respect Abi's wishes, but he didn't know if he would be able to stay away from Kevin.

Becca had called to find out what was going on. Her voicemail said that officers had arrived at the pub and arrested Kevin. Henry couldn't face talking to her so he texted her and told her everything was all right. He promised to call her in the morning and explain. Eventually, he was allowed to join Abi in her private room.

The police liaison officer was sitting on a chair in

the corner of the room. Abi was sitting on the side of the bed. Her wrist was bandaged and the bruising on her neck was already darker than before. Her face was red and puffy from crying and she had stitches in her eye. He approached her slowly. "How are you feeling?"

She shrugged.

"I'm so sorry, Abigail. I let this happen to you. It's all my fault." He couldn't hold back any longer. Tears began to stream down his cheeks.

"No, Henry." She held her hand out to him and he wrapped his arms around her. She was still shaking. He promised himself that he would never let anyone – or anything – hurt her again.

After a few minutes he broke the embrace and fixed his eyes on the stitches by her eye. He tried his hardest not to cry again. He had to be strong for her.

"I'm all right, Henry. It's just a sprained wrist. A few bruises. Nothing that won't heal." She broke his gaze and looked down at the floor. Although she felt physically numb, there was a different kind of pain on the inside, one she knew would never heal.

He caught her eye and gave her a little smile. "You're so brave, Abigail. I know you're going to be OK. And you're not on your own. I'm here for you." He turned to the police officer. "So, what happens next?"

"Mr Preston is too drunk for questioning, so they'll let him sober up in a cell and question him in the morning. He'll most likely get a solicitor, then be formally charged. There's a good probability that he'll be released under caution."

"Released? Are you kidding?"

"I'm sorry. There's a process we have to follow." She looked at Abi. "We will issue him a Domestic Violence Protection Notice, or DVPN for short. This means, if Mr Preston is released, he cannot return to the family home. You and your daughter will be safe there. On Monday we will go to court and get a Domestic Violence Protection Order or DVPO from the magistrate. This means that your husband won't be able to make any kind of contact with you for twenty-eight days. If he does, he'll be arrested."

"Twenty-eight days?" Henry snapped. "What the hell is she meant to do after that? That animal will be free. What if he hurts her again? And Emma. Does this order cover her too?"

"Yes, the order covers her too. We take children's welfare very seriously, sir."

"Very seriously? Yeah, sounds like it. Look at what he's done to her and you're just—"

"Will you both stop talking about me like I'm not here?" Abi snapped.

Henry turned back to her and took her hand. He cradled it in his. "I'm so sorry. You're right. Why don't you try and sleep for a few hours?"

"I can't sleep. I need to get home to Emma." She looked at the officer. "Can I go now?"

"I'll have to check with the doctor—"

But Abi was already getting up. "I need to get my daughter out of that house. Now."

Chapter Sixteen

It was just before 6 a.m. when Abi and Henry arrived back at the house. Abi headed straight upstairs to check on Emma. She opened the bedroom door and crept in. When she saw Emma tucked up in bed, safe and secure, she began to cry again. She watched her for a few moments, knowing that when she woke up her life would change forever. She wanted to shield her as much as possible from what was going to happen, but it was inevitable that there would be hard times ahead. When she left the room, she closed the door quietly behind her then leaned against it and wiped the tears from her eyes.

It was time for her to take her life back.

On her way back downstairs, she met Henry coming out of the living room.

"Your neighbour is asleep on the sofa. But you can probably hear that for yourself." He drew his hand to his ear.

Abi stopped to listen. She could hear Mrs Smith snoring from behind the closed door. She cracked a smile.

Henry smiled too. "You should probably have a shower and change your clothes." He pointed to the bloodstains on her dress. Abi's body tensed. The painkillers and tiredness had taken her mind off the pain; she'd been on autopilot and hadn't thought to look at herself in a mirror. She probably looked dreadful, but she didn't care. There were more pressing matters.

"OK, in a minute. We don't have much time. I need your bank account number and the sort code."

He reached into his pocket for his wallet but gave her a confused look.

"The house, money, cars – everything's in Kevin's name. He is not going to let me have a penny. I'll have to transfer as much cash as I can before he's sober enough to think about it. Can you hold on to it for me until I get myself sorted out?"

"Of course."

She left him in the hall and hurried to the cloakroom. After a few seconds she returned with her car keys, two credit cards, her debit card and a note of their PINs. "There's a service station at the end of the road. After I have a shower, I want you to go there and fill the car with diesel and go to the ATM and withdraw as much cash as you can from each card. Then come back here and help me pack."

"Pack? No, that's not right. You don't have to leave your home."

"I don't want to be here when he's released."

"It's OK. You have that protection notice, and tomorrow it'll be an order. He can't come near you. This is your home, and Emma's."

"No. It *was* our home. But we're leaving here today, and I never want to set foot in this place again."

"OK, but only if you're completely sure. You can stay with me. I'll tell Becca I can't have Toby for a while. You can have my room and Emma can have his. I'll sleep on the sofa."

As much as she would have loved that, it wasn't the right time. She wanted to be with her family. She ran her hand down his arm. "Thank you, Henry. That's very sweet, but I can't. I'll go to my sister's. Evie will be able to squeeze us in until I get something sorted out."

His heart sank. Milton Keynes was nearly a three-hour round trip. "But what will you do about school?"

"It's only two weeks until the summer holidays. She won't fall behind too much." She glanced at the living-room door. "I can't stay here. And I need you to promise me something."

"Anything."

"I want you to stay away from Kevin."

He shook his head. "That's the only promise I can't make."

"I mean it. I don't want you coming here and causing any trouble. And if you see him around town, please just walk away."

"I've got to be honest with you. I don't think I can do that. Not after what he did to you."

"Promise me, Henry! The last thing we need is for you to get into trouble with the police. You'll lose your job."

He was taken aback at her choice of words. Had she meant to say we?

"Let's get moving."

He looked at her in amazement. How was she even functioning, never mind taking control of the situation? Maybe it was the adrenaline taking over, or she was still in shock. Either way, he knew that she was going to be OK.

After a quick shower, Abi hunted for the polo-neck jumper she had bought a few months ago. It was the only thing that would conceal her bruises. She put on her most comfortable jeans and a pair of trainers, then examined herself in the mirror. The bruises on her neck were hardly noticeable and the sleeve of the jumper almost covered the bandage on her wrist. But no amount of make-up, or sunglasses, would hide the bruising around her eye. How would she explain it to Emma? To anyone?

When she got back downstairs, Henry left to go to the ATM. She locked the door behind him then looked around the hall. She could remember buying the doormat, the curtains and every piece of furniture in the house. She had chosen every photo and every picture on the walls, trying her hardest to make the house into a home. Henry was right; she shouldn't have to leave her home, but she wanted to. She choked back her tears. She loved this house, but she hadn't been truly happy here, not for a long time.

She'd never be able to set foot in her living room again without reliving what had happened there. She knew she would never feel safe here again. She tried not to dwell too much on her heartache. She had her sister, Henry and Glenda to turn to. She was lucky. There were many other women in a similar situation who weren't so lucky.

Back in her bedroom, she packed a small bag with her favourite things. Then she started to make piles of items on the bed: designer clothes, coats, shoes, handbags, most of which still had the labels on. During the last few years she'd mainly shopped out of boredom, or to spend money when Kevin had insisted. She'd bought frivolous things she knew she would never need. But she needed those things now. She thought she might be able to sell them online – they should fetch quite a bit, and that would help to keep her and Emma afloat financially, at least in the short term. She was gathering her jewellery when she heard noises in Emma's room.

She was awake.

Abi crept into her room.

Emma gasped when she saw Abi's bruised eye and bandaged wrist. "Mummy…" Her voice was shaky.

"It's OK, sweetheart." Abi tried to make herself sound upbeat. "Everything is OK. Silly Mummy just fell down the stairs."

Emma covered her mouth and laughed. "Silly Mummy."

Abi sat on the side of Emma's bed and took her hand. "Today is going to be a busy day. I need you to pack all of your favourite things because we're going to go and stay with Auntie Evie for a while."

"Yay!" Emma clapped her hands. "All of us? Daddy too?"

"Not Daddy, sweetheart. He has to work, so he's going to stay here."

Emma folded her arms and pouted.

"I know, sweetheart. I'm going to miss him too." The words almost stuck in her throat. "But think of all the fun you'll have staying with your cousins for a while."

"What about school?"

"Don't worry about boring old school!" Abi made a funny face. "I'll tell your teacher we're going on an adventure. She's going to be jealous."

Emma nodded. "Really jealous, Mummy!"

When Henry got back, he helped Emma to pack her bags then took her to Becca's to spend the rest of the morning with Toby. Steve followed him, in his own car, to help with the move. Mrs Smith made everyone breakfast while they spent the morning packing the cars with Abi's clothes and other expensive items from the house. Abi packed their birth certificates, passports and other important documentation, some photographs and a few keepsakes. She made a final pass through the house to make sure she hadn't forgotten anything. In the kitchen, she found Kevin's glass from the night before, drying on the draining board. She went into the utility room to Kevin's drinks cupboard and selected a brand-new bottle of Jack Daniels. She placed the bottle and the glass on the dinner table at Kevin's usual seat. A little smile crossed her face as she took off her wedding and engagement rings and set them beside the bottle. That was her last act as a married woman.

It was time to go. Abi locked the front door then posted her key through the letterbox. She turned to Mrs Smith and took her hands. "Thank you for everything. You have my number – please keep in touch."

"I will, dear. You take care of yourself and that beautiful little girl." She squeezed Abi's hands tightly.

"I will. And promise me you won't say anything about any of this to Kevin when he gets back. Just act normal, as if you don't know anything about what happened. It'll be easier in the long run."

Mrs Smith sighed and shook her head. "Don't worry, dear. I'll be keeping my distance from that man."

"Good. Take care." Abi gave Mrs Smith a long hug and a kiss on the cheek. She took one last look at the house. When Kevin had bought it, she'd been so happy and full of hope for their future. Part of her felt that she was wrong to leave it, but the other part felt nothing but relief.

***

Henry pulled the SUV into Becca's driveway and switched off the engine. Shocked by the events of the last few hours, they sat for a few minutes in silence.

"Do you want to come in with me?" he asked finally.

She shook her head. "No. We always go to Evelyn's on Sunday for lunch so she'll be expecting us. But I want to give her a call first. I just can't turn up on her doorstep like this. And I need to warn her not to make a fuss in front of Emma. I want to shield her from this as much as possible."

Henry watched as she cradled her bandaged wrist. He would have given anything to take her pain away, but he knew that wasn't possible. All he could do for her, and Emma, was be there, whatever they needed. He gave her knee a reassuring squeeze. "OK. I'll give you a few minutes before I bring Emma out."

"Thank you." Abi waited until he and Steve had gone into the house before she got her phone from her bag and called Evelyn. She tried to stop herself from shaking as she waited for her sister to answer.

"Hi..." She went silent. She didn't know what to say.

"Abi? Are you there?"

"Yes ... I'm just ... letting you know that we're running late but we're on our way."

"That's OK. I'm running late too. We all slept late and had a really lazy morning. Is that what you two did?"

"Um-hm." Abi choked.

"Abi?" Evelyn's voice was hesitant. "Are you OK? Is there something wrong?"

"Yes."

"What is it?"

"Something's happened. I've left Kevin. Is it all right if Emma and I stay with you for a while?"

"Of course it's all right!" Evelyn exclaimed. "Stay as long as you like. But what happened?"

"I got hurt. I ... I don't want you to worry when you see me." Abi's voice broke. "Please don't make a fuss in front of Emma."

"Abi?"

She tried to keep her voice level. "I'll explain when I get there. See you soon." She ended the call and put the phone back into her bag. She pulled down the sun visor and examined her eye and neck in the mirror. Never had she imagined having to explain anything like this.

Henry drove Abi and Emma to Milton Keynes in the SUV while Steve followed in his own car. Henry tried to concentrate on the road, but his eyes kept drifting to Abi. She was so still. Just staring out of the window in silence. His mind was in overdrive: he still couldn't believe what was happening. The night before had been surreal. One minute he'd been on a date with Colette, and the next he was in a hospital with Abi and a police escort. He was wondering what tomorrow would bring when Emma burst out singing. She was watching *Frozen* on the headrest DVD player. He looked over at Abi. She had turned her head and was watching Emma intently. He thought he saw a little smile cross her face.

***

Evelyn opened the front door and gasped in horror. "Abi!"

"It's OK, Auntie Evie," Emma said. "Silly Mummy

just fell down the stairs." She pushed past her aunt and ran into the house to find her cousins.

Dumbstruck, Evelyn watched her go, then turned back to Abi. They stared at one another in silence. Both had tears in their eyes. After a few seconds, Evelyn held her hand out to Abi and brought her into the house.

Emma played with her cousins while Abi and Evelyn talked. Although Evelyn tried desperately to be strong for her younger sister, she couldn't help breaking down into tears when Abi told her what had happened last night. She told her about the meal and the fight they'd had afterwards. That Kevin had accused her of cheating and threatened to take away her things and make her a prisoner in her own home. Then Abi went silent.

"It's OK. We don't have to do this now."

"I want to tell you. I need to tell you. To make it real." She looked down at the floor. "He punched me in the stomach. It hurt so much that I fell. Then he grabbed my throat. He squeezed so hard, I couldn't breathe. I thought he was going to strangle me. I tried to fight him off, but he was too strong. I closed my eyes and prayed that he would stop. I begged him. Then he punched me in the face. I fell to the floor, and he kicked me. Six, maybe seven times. It felt like it would never end, but I suppose it only lasted a few seconds. Then there was nothing. I was afraid to move. I just lay on the floor until I heard the front door close. I didn't know where he was going, or when he'd be back. So I just lay there. Time passed – I don't know how long it was before I got up. I went into the kitchen. I sat at the table and I just … I didn't know what to do."

Tears rolled down Evelyn's face. "Please tell me you called the police."

"Not at first. I was afraid to move. To do anything. I was frightened that he'd come back and do it again. Or worse. I've never seen him like that. He had this awful look in his eyes. I thought he was going to kill me." She was trembling. "Then by some miracle, Henry arrived at my door. If he hadn't, I honestly don't know what I would have done. Or what Kevin would have done when he came back."

"Who's Henry?"

"A friend. He's the one who brought me here."

"Is he the man Kevin thought you were having an affair with?"

She nodded. "I wasn't. At least ... I don't know. Maybe I was. We didn't sleep together; we've never even kissed. But we spent time together. We shopped, we decorated, we did things that Kevin and I never did together. I enjoyed every minute I spent with him. And I didn't tell Kevin about him. I knew what he would say." She lowered her head. "Is that an affair?"

Evelyn wrapped her arms around Abi. "I don't know. But it's no excuse for what Kevin did to you. Did you call the police, eventually?"

"Yes. Kevin's been arrested. But I don't know what's going to happen next..." She began to sob. "I don't know what to do."

"It's OK. You don't have to know right now. We'll figure it out. But whatever happens, you have me and Javid. We're here for you, and you can stay here as long as you want." She squeezed Abi tightly. "Why didn't you call me? I'd have come down, stayed with you, made sure that Kevin was the one to leave."

Abi pulled away from Evelyn. "No. I had to leave." She got up from the sofa and looked out of the window at Henry and Steve, who were still sitting in her car.

"Henry and his friend helped me bring my things. I'm never going back to that house."

Evelyn joined her at the window. "Then we'd better get the kettle on and offer them some tea."

After some awkward introductions over a pot of tea, Henry and Steve unpacked the cars. Evelyn's husband, Javid, cleared some space in the garage and sorted out somewhere for Abi and Emma to sleep. Abi wanted to keep everything as normal as possible for Emma, so while they discussed the practicalities of their new situation Abi helped Evelyn prepare Sunday lunch. Using the potato peeler with her bandaged wrist was a struggle. Evie sighed and took it from her. She pointed to a seat at the table. "Sit. There's a bottle of wine in the fridge. Why don't you pour us both a glass?"

"I don't want wine. Stop fussing, Evelyn. All I need is a pen and some paper. I need to make a list of everything I need to do."

"You and your lists." Evelyn pointed to a notepad and pen magnetised to the fridge. "You're so organised, just like Dad used to be." Then she drew a sharp breath. "What are we going to do about Mum? *He* pays for her nursing home. I don't know if Javid and I can afford to help with the cost."

Abi's heart sank. She hadn't given her mum a second thought. Moving her to a new nursing home would confuse and unsettle her, but there was nothing else they could do. "We'll have to start looking for somewhere else for her to go. I'll make that the second thing on my to-do list tomorrow."

"What's the first thing?"

"To find a solicitor. And I have to go back to the police station to make an official statement and fill out the paperwork for some order. I think they said something about seeing a judge too. I can't remember. It's all a blur."

Evelyn rested her hand on Abi's shoulder. "Don't worry, we're here for you. Anything you need."

Abi sighed. The only thing she needed was for them to lock Kevin up and throw away the key. She had no idea that last night would be the only night Kevin would spend in custody.

Evelyn insisted that Henry and Steve stayed for Sunday lunch – which, given the time of day, was now dinner. Javid put down a blanket and some cushions in the conservatory for the children, who were happy – and noisy – with their picnic-style meal. The mood in the kitchen was much more sombre. The adults sat at the table in silence. Abi looked around at them all, exchanging polite nods and smiles. She rubbed her eyes. Was this going to be her life from now on? Would people be tiptoeing around her forever? Afraid to be themselves in case they upset her? Unable to tolerate the sympathetic looks any longer, Abi placed her knife and fork on the table. "Evie, I think I will have that glass of wine."

Evelyn smiled and elbowed Javid in the ribs. He jumped up and went to fetch the wine and some glasses. He placed a full glass in front of each sister and raised his eyebrows at Henry and Steve. Both shook their heads silently. Abi tutted. "Has everyone forgotten how to make small talk?"

Henry smiled at her and took the lead. "Anyone read any good books lately?"

After dinner they chatted over tea and coffee for a

while until Steve checked the time on his phone and gave Henry a nudge. "It's getting late. We've got school in the morning – we'd better make a move."

Henry glanced at Abi. "Actually, I'm going to find a hotel nearby. In case Abigail needs me in the morning."

Abi smiled at him. "That's very sweet, but life goes on. You have to go to work. Don't worry, Evelyn and Javid will look after me."

His face dropped. "But—"

"No buts, Henry," she said firmly.

"OK, then. I'll nip in and say goodbye to Emma." He got up from the table and left the kitchen. Abi watched him go. She knew she'd upset him, but she didn't have time to worry about that now. She needed to focus on herself and Emma.

Steve had already said his goodbyes and was waiting in the car. Reluctant to leave, Henry lingered at the front door with Abi. "Are you sure you don't want me to stay at a hotel? It's no trouble. What if Kevin shows up?"

"He won't. There's that order against him. And if he's stupid enough to ignore it, Javid is here, and we'll call the police. Please don't take this the wrong way. I'm so grateful for everything you've done for me, but I just need to be with my family right now."

Henry couldn't bear it. She was going through so much heartbreak; he desperately wanted to stay and make sure she was all right. Surely she knew how he felt about her? It was breaking his heart that she was sending him away. But he tried not to fall apart in front of her. "I understand."

"Thank you." She took his hands and gazed into his eyes. "This isn't goodbye, Henry. I just need some time to … make sense of my life again."

The relief her words gave him was immense. Not knowing how long it would be until he saw her again, he looked longingly at her, trying to memorise every detail – until Steve beeped the car horn. Henry shot a dirty look at him then turned back to Abi. "Goodnight. Try to get some sleep." He let go of her hands and made his way towards Steve's car.

Abi held back her tears. Letting him leave was the right thing to do, but watching him walk away down the driveway was more painful than she'd thought it would be. She didn't want him to leave, especially like this. He was at the gate when she called to him.

"Henry!"

He stopped in his tracks and turned to see her walking towards him.

"Text me to let me know you got home safely." She leaned in close and planted a kiss on his cheek.

"I will. Goodnight, Abigail." He waited until she'd gone into the house and closed the door before he got into the car. He ran his hand over his cheek where she'd kissed it and couldn't help smiling.

That had been their first kiss.

***

Earlier that afternoon, when Kevin had been deemed sober enough, he was permitted to make his one phone call. He rang his father, gave him his version of events and instructed him to find a good solicitor. Money was no object. Back in his cell, he waited with nothing but his hangover for company until an officer took him to an interview room. The clock on the wall had stopped and his watch and phone had been taken, so he had no idea of the exact time. He hadn't been able to stomach the watery stew he'd been given for lunch. What he wouldn't give for one of Abi's fry-ups. The thought of her made his blood boil. He clenched his fists. *I should have known she'd do something petty like this. I shouldn't have left her in the house, but I couldn't stand the sound of her crying any more. And over what? A few slaps. Wait until I get my hands on her. I'll really give her something to cry about.*

Just then, the door opened. Kevin looked up to see a tall, slim man approach the table. He was a few years older than him and had short brown hair, a clean-shaven face and wore a very expensive suit. He placed his gleaming briefcase on the table and extended his hand. "My name is Jonathan Christian. Your father has retained my services."

Kevin nodded and shook his solicitor's hand. His head was thumping, but he could tell by Christian's appearance and manner that he meant business.

"Have you been treated well? Fed and watered?"

Kevin nodded again.

"Good. OK." He pulled out a chair and sat down. "My job here is to limit the damage and ensure you get the best possible result. In order for that to happen, you have to trust me one hundred per cent. You must answer all my questions truthfully and do exactly as instructed. OK?"

"OK."

"Good. When I bring the police officers in, they will inform you why you are here, then ask you some questions. You will confirm your name, age and address. Your answer to all subsequent questions will be 'no comment'. Understood?"

"Yes."

"OK. You will probably be charged this evening.

Unfortunately, there's no getting away from that, but I should be able to get you out of here tonight. I have been informed that your wife and daughter have left the family home, so you are free to return there. You are not permitted to contact either of them in any way. If you do, you will end up back here with another charge – and you will need to find new representation. I will not tolerate a client ignoring my instructions and making matters worse for himself. I will organise a taxi and you will go straight home." He reached into the inside pocket of his suit jacket and produced a gold card-holder. He slid a business card across the table to Kevin. "I want you in my office at 9 a.m. tomorrow, sober and well dressed. Understood?"

"Yes."

"OK. Don't look so scared." He rubbed his hands. "Let's do this!" He got up from his chair and strode across the room, then opened the door. "We're ready," he said to the officer waiting outside.

It was dusk by the time Kevin returned to what he knew would be an empty house. He picked Abi's keys up off the mat and put them on the hall table. He stared at the aged oak table and remembered how excited she had been when she ordered it, and how she couldn't wait for it to arrive. He walked across the marble-floored hall to the kitchen: the kitchen she had spent three whole days planning with the kitchen designer, and which had cost him a small fortune. Straight away he noticed the bottle of Jack Daniels and the glass waiting at his place at the table, but it was only when he sat down that he saw Abi's wedding and engagement rings on the placemat beside the bottle. He picked up the rings and stared at them. *What kind of game is she playing? She*

knows these are expensive. And why did she leave the house? I was expecting her to fight for it. She'll definitely fight for half my money – more than half, but there's no way she's going to get it. That guy Christian seems to know what he's doing. Dad made a good choice. Dad!
He reached for the bottle and poured himself a large drink. His parents would have questions for him; he'd have to direct their attention towards Abi's affair and keep the details of the assault vague. He hadn't hit her that hard, he reasoned. She was just using it as an excuse to get out of the marriage. He downed the drink in one, then took Abi's rings to the sink and placed them carefully in the little crystal saucer she always kept them in when she was cleaning. He went back to the table, picked up the glass and the bottle, then took them upstairs.

He went into Emma's bedroom and sat down on the bed. He poured himself another drink. *What has she done to me? Spending the night in a cell was bad, but not as bad as being arrested in the pub in front of everyone. It's probably already all over town. And what about my job? What if my boss hears about this? I'll have to make them see that I'm not an abuser. She drove me to it. She lied to me and cheated, made me a laughing stock. I'm a good husband and provider. She threw it back in my face. She made me hit her. But why did she have to overreact and go to the police? It was just a few slaps. It's the only time I've hit her. But she's burned her bridges. I'm not going to try and get her back or grovel for forgiveness, but I'm not done with the bitch yet.*

Chapter Seventeen

The night before, Javid had planned for his two daughters to bunk in together so that Abi and Emma could share the single bed in their youngest's room. But the cousins hatched a plan to sneak Emma in with them during the night. Abi pretended not to notice them smuggle her out. She knew Emma would enjoy the company, and she could definitely do with the sleep herself. But she didn't sleep. She tossed and turned all night.

In the morning, she lay in bed and listened to Evelyn and Javid getting their children ready for school. She could hear Emma's voice amid the commotion. She was laughing and carrying on with her cousins, obviously relishing the fact that she didn't have to go to school herself – she was on a special holiday. It wasn't until Abi heard the front door close that she felt brave enough to get out of bed. She sat on the side of the bed and tried to summon the energy to put on her slippers and dressing gown. Not sure who had taken the children to school, Abi crept downstairs and was relieved to find Emma in the kitchen with Evelyn.

Evelyn greeted her with a smile and a long hug. She didn't comment on how dreadful Abi knew she must look. "The kettle is on. And we've got fruit, toast and cereal."

"Just tea, thanks." She looked over at Emma, who was so engrossed in a game on her eldest cousin's Nintendo Switch that she hadn't even noticed Abi coming into the kitchen. It looked like she wasn't too suspicious so far. This gave Abi some comfort – hope that things would be all right. But now was not the time to relax; she had a lot to do. "Evie, can I use your laptop? I have to check my bank account." There was a daily limit to the amount she could transfer out, and she thought she might be able to withdraw some more. The night before, after Henry had left, she had received a phone call from her police liaison officer to inform her that Kevin had been released. He would probably have frozen the account already, but she had to try. Evelyn pointed to the laptop, which sat on the sideboard.

Abi logged on to her internet banking then groaned in exasperation. "He's emptied my account and the house account. I don't know how." She rubbed her temples. She had only been able to gather a total of £3,500 from her cards and accounts. That wasn't much for her and Emma to live on. How long would it last? She had no idea how long it would take to claim benefits and come to a financial agreement with Kevin. Evelyn and Javid would only be able to help her in the short term.

There was a knock on the front door. Abi looked at Evelyn. "Please don't let that be Kevin!"

"It can't be! You stay here." Evelyn gave her a panicked look and went to answer the door.

Abi crept to the kitchen door and strained to listen. A male voice – and it wasn't Kevin's. Just as she went to sit back down at the table, Evelyn came into the kitchen. "There's two policemen at the door. Kevin's reported your car as stolen."

Abi groaned and followed Evelyn to the front door. The two male police officers standing there exchanged a concerned look when they saw Abi's eye, which was bruised and swollen.

"My name is Abigail Preston." She pointed to the SUV. "Kevin Preston's name might be on the paperwork, but that is my car. My husband gave it to me for my birthday." She pointed to her eye. "He gave me this on Saturday night. That's why I had to get away from him, with my daughter. He's obviously petty and bitter and wants to harass me. But if you wait here for a minute, I will get you the keys and you can take what he considers his property back to him. I don't need it any more. I'm safe here with my sister."

The older of the two officers shook his head. "That won't be necessary, Mrs Preston. You can hold on to the car. The division of marital assets is not in our remit – that's something that should be done through your solicitor. Excuse me, but I need to ask. Have you reported the incident?"

"Yes, to my local station. My husband was arrested on Saturday night and released yesterday evening. I have a DV something notice and there's something to come from court today."

"That'll be the DVPO. Is there anything else we can do for you at this time?"

"No. Thank you."

"Then we're sorry to have disturbed you. I will put a note on the system so we don't bother you again about the car." The officer reached into his pocket and produced a business card, which he offered to Abi. "This is our number. You're a long way from your local station. If you would like our family liaison officer to come over and discuss anything with you, just call. And if by any chance your husband is foolish enough to come here and cause any trouble, give us a call and we'll send someone over immediately to arrest him."

"Thank you." She took the card and closed the

door.

"I can't believe him!" Evelyn said as she turned back to the kitchen. "That'll be the start of it. I suspect there's worse to come." She looked over her shoulder at Abi and found her crouching on the floor, her back against the door. She was shaking and taking giant panicky breaths. Evelyn helped her up and into the living room.

"I can't do this." Abi sat down on the sofa and buried her head in her hands. "I can't. I can't."

Evelyn rubbed her hand in circles on Abi's back to soothe her. "Of course you can. You handled that brilliantly. I had no idea you were so strong. You can do this. People will be on your side."

"But the car, the bank accounts – what else is he going to do? And when will Mum's nursing home call to say he hasn't paid? Oh shit. I need to call the nursing home." She jumped up and ran to the kitchen table, where she'd left her mobile phone. There were no bars. She held it up and waved it at Evelyn. "There's no signal. I bet he's had it cut off." She pointed to Emma. "Look after her. I need some fresh air." She hurried out of the kitchen and went upstairs to get dressed.

She threw on the jeans and jumper she'd worn the day before and reached for her trainers. Trying to hold back the tears, she tied the laces and hurried down the stairs. She called into the kitchen, "I'll be back in half an hour." Then she ran out of the front door. The police car was still parked on the street outside the house. She nodded to the officers as she passed, then hurried down the street. It was only a short distance from Evelyn's house to a river that had a path beside it. She couldn't get there fast enough.

As she walked, she tried to organise her to-do list.

Police station. Solicitor. Mum. Emma. Bank accounts. Divorce. Benefits. School. The car. There had to be things she hadn't thought about yet. Immersed in her thoughts, she didn't notice that people were looking at her strangely. Then she remembered her eye. She lowered her head and upped her pace. It wouldn't be possible to do everything today, or this week. Maybe not even this month. How many months would it take? She didn't realise how fast or how far she had walked until she reached a small gate. Overwhelmed, she spotted a bench and took a seat to catch her breath. She needed to take things one day at a time. That's all she could do. She took a few deep breaths and got up, intending to turn back to the house. Then she saw a man running towards her. *Is that Kevin?* He was wearing jogging gear, the likes of which Kevin would never be seen dead in, but he was the same height, the same build, and was coming straight towards her. *No, it can't be.* She stood perfectly still as the man drew closer, then he just jogged past her. She sank back down on the bench. The police had said he'd be arrested if he came anywhere near her. Kevin would know that too. She knew him – there was no way he would risk getting into any more trouble with the police. And there was no way he would grovel to her to try to win her around. His pride and stubbornness wouldn't let him. She sat on the bench for a few more minutes before she headed back to the house, taking deep breaths and vowing to take things one day at a time.

***

Abi had been right about Kevin. At 9 a.m. he was at the offices of Christian and McKendry, sipping a fancy coffee. He was sober, clean-shaven and wearing one of his most expensive suits. His solicitor looked impressed. "Like I said yesterday, you need to trust me and be honest. There's no judgement here, I promise you. Let's get started. Talk me through the events of Saturday night."

"It all happened so fast. We were out enjoying dinner together when one of her friends saw us and came over to our table for a chat. She let it slip that Abs was having an affair. I was shocked. Mortified. I couldn't believe it. We've been married for six wonderful years, we have a beautiful daughter and a lovely home. Why on earth would she need someone else? I was beside myself. When we got home, she admitted it to me. Said she didn't love me, she loved him, and she was going to leave me and never let me see my daughter again. She was goading me, trying to wind me up. I don't know what happened. I just snapped."

"Had you been drinking?"

"Yes."

"How much?"

"A lot."

"OK. Carry on."

"She tried to hit me. That's why I grabbed her wrist – to stop her. Then she said she was leaving me and taking my daughter. I was beside myself. I just saw red. Before I knew what was happening, I'd hit her."

Jonathan Christian was scribbling notes while he listened. "How many times?"

"Once or twice."

"What was it? Once or twice?"

"Twice."

"What did you use?"

"Pardon me?"

"Your fist, belt, something else?"

"My fist."

"Anything else?"

"She fell onto the floor and ... I kicked her."

"How many times?"

"I don't know. More than once, not that many."

"Anything else?"

Kevin shook his head.

"How long did the assault last?"

The word 'assault' hit him like a ton of bricks. It wasn't an assault; it was just a few slaps. This was way out of control. "A few seconds – it couldn't have been more than a minute. But I was out of my mind."

"Is this the first time you have assaulted your wife?"

"The first time. I swear. I loved my wife, I gave her everything. That's the problem – that's why it hurt so much to find out she was having an affair. But I'm done with that bitch. And I don't want her getting my house – or my money. She cheated on me. She doesn't deserve a penny."

"OK. This is what we're going to do. This is how you dress. Every day. No drinking in public. And absolutely no calling your wife a bitch outside this office. You behave impeccably and whether you feel remorse or not, you will *show* remorse for your actions. Tell anyone who'll listen how sorry you are. This is damage limitation. We need to make clear that this was an isolated incident, brought about by your rage at hearing about your wife's affair. Like you say, you were out of your mind with jealousy and you were drunk – people aren't in control when they're drunk. My assistant will give you the name of an anger management counsellor and you will attend weekly sessions. You'll also seek advice from your GP about your drinking – I don't care whether you use it or not. Perhaps when you're there you could mention that you've been having trouble sleeping. You feel guilty and anxious – maybe you need anxiety medication. This will all go on your medical record and will look well for you with the judge. You will, of course, plead guilty to the assault, but we can claim diminished responsibility. It was an isolated incident. You're sorry, and you've taken all these steps to ensure that it never happens again." He made a few more notes then turned to a new page. "Will you be seeking a reconciliation with Mrs Preston?"

Kevin shook his head.

"Right. I have scheduled a 9.30 meeting for you with my esteemed colleague, Mr McKendry. He can handle your divorce and will advise you on the best course of action regarding custody of your daughter. While it's not my specialty, I would imagine that with a charge of domestic assault it won't be easy to get any sort of custody, but there's few better than Mr McKendry if you want to fight for it."

"I haven't even thought about custody yet." Kevin mulled it over quickly. Any type of custody would mean he'd be at Emma's beck and call. He'd have to take her to school, cook for her, clean up after her. It might mean losing his weekends. But he didn't want to come across as an unsympathetic father, not even to his solicitor. He lowered his head. "Obviously I would love to fight for custody, but I understand that Emma is better off with her mother. I've caused enough trouble for my family. Even though not being able to see her every day will kill me, I'll have to make do with whatever I can get."

Jonathan Christian made a few more notes then

closed the file. "That's all I need from you this morning. If you would like to take a seat in reception, my assistant will give you some paperwork to fill in while you wait for Mr McKendry."

That's it? Dumbstruck, Kevin remained seated while Mr Christian swapped his file for another on his desk. He waited for a few seconds then slowly pushed his chair back and stood up. "Can I ask you one more question?"

"Certainly," came the curt response.

"Will I go to prison?"

"Do exactly as I say, and it will be unlikely. I've had some very successful results with far worse cases."

"Thank you." Kevin shook hands with his solicitor and smiled to himself as he walked to the door. Jonathan Christian *did* know what he was doing. His dad had been right to hire him. Things were looking up.

***

Abi's day wasn't as positive. Evelyn drove them back to Grovewood and dropped Emma off at Glenda's house before taking Abi to the police station.

Evelyn remained in the waiting room until Abi and her solicitor had finished speaking with the officers. When Abi came out to reception with her coat and bag, Evelyn held her arms out for a hug. "How did it go?"

"Ugh. All right, I think. But I want to get out of here. I'll tell you in the car."

"The solicitor that Javid's brother recommended was lovely. She assured me that I have a very strong case and things will work out in my favour, but I still feel anxious. Then I gave my official statement and had some more pictures taken of my bruises."

"I hope you didn't forget the ones on your back?"

"Of course I didn't!"

"Sorry. Then what happened?"

"The family officer gave me some numbers to ring. They talked about a women's shelter, but thankfully I don't need that because I have you." She grabbed Evelyn's hand and squeezed it tight. "There are some women's groups I can call – they can give me advice about the next steps. You know, benefits, housing … counselling. And I have to get a separate solicitor to handle the divorce." She buried her head in her hands. "There's so much. It's confusing. And I'm so tired."

"Did you sleep at all last night?"

"I may have drifted off for a few minutes, but nothing substantial."

"We have some super-strong painkillers left over from when Javid had his back injury last year. Two of them made him so drowsy, he had no trouble sleeping. Take one tonight, and tomorrow I'll try and get you an appointment with my GP and see if there's something she can give you to help you relax. To stop feeling anxious."

Abi's shoulders tensed. "I don't want to take medication. Not again."

"It helped you deal with your postnatal depression and it will help you deal with this. You got stitches in your eye to help that heal – this is exactly the same thing."

Abi tutted and got her phone from her bag. "I should text Glenda – tell her we're on our way."

"Don't you want to pop over and see Henry for a few minutes?"

"No … I'll phone him later."

"I saw the way he was staring at you over the dinner table yesterday. He's totally in love with you. I know it's early days, but—"

"Leave it, Evelyn!" Abi snapped. "Jumping into bed with Henry isn't going to fix everything that's wrong with my life." After everything that had happened, she wasn't even sure if what she felt about Henry was real. Had she imagined her feelings because he was nice and made her feel good about herself? Or worse, was she using him as a form of validation because she was unhappy? She needed space to clear her head. If there was anything real between them, it would come. In time. If Henry really did care about her, he would give her the space she asked for.

Evelyn glanced at Abi out of the corner of her eye. She hadn't seen her react so passionately to anything in years. That's when it dawned on her: Kevin had broken Abi's spirit. He'd done it so gradually that she hadn't even noticed the change in her own sister. She was overcome with guilt. She wanted to make up for it by helping Abi in any way she could. "I didn't mean anything by it, I just meant he seems nice. Anyway, do you want me to phone the kids' school in the morning and see if Emma can go there for the rest of the term?"

"Why? It's only two weeks."

"Yes, but if you want her to go there next year it'll be a little taster for her. Let her know what to expect."

Abi bowed her head. Evelyn might love to have her and Emma living closer, but Abi hadn't decided whether or not she was going to stay in Milton Keynes. She had given up her house because of Kevin, but she wasn't sure she could give up her home, her friends and Emma's friends. She'd never lived anywhere other than

Grovewood, and she didn't want to. It was full of happy memories of her childhood and of her mum and dad – and Henry lived there too. But living there would mean being close to Kevin, and she wasn't sure if she could handle that.

Chapter Eighteen

Over the next few weeks, and countless sleepless nights, Abi had good days and bad. Some days she was able not to dwell on what happened and focused all her energy on getting Kevin out of her life and building a new one for her and Emma. Other days, it was difficult for her to find a reason to get out of bed. She suffered bouts of anxiety and was overcome by feelings of hopelessness, anger and regret. She had completely recovered from her physical injuries, but she had a different kind of injury that she was reluctant to address.

Evelyn finally persuaded Abi to make an appointment to see her own GP. Abi only agreed to get Evelyn off her back, but the appointment went very differently to what she had expected. Once she started talking, she couldn't stop. The doctor listened as Abi poured her heart out – not only about Kevin and what had happened, but about the loss of her father, her mother's health, and her own postnatal depression. The doctor suggested referring her for counselling and, much to her own surprise, Abi agreed immediately. She also agreed to let Emma talk to a children's counsellor. She hadn't wanted Emma to have to see a counsellor, but Abi was beginning to accept that it was a vital part of the healing process. Emma was becoming increasingly upset and angry at Abi for not letting her go home to see her daddy. Most of the time she was happy at her cousins' house because she was so used to spending time there without Kevin, but every now and then she begged Abi to take her home. She said she missed her bedroom, her friends and most of all her daddy. Abi wasn't equipped to explain or help a five-year-old through something like this; she could hardly get to grips with it herself.

Just when Abi thought her life couldn't get any more surreal, she received word from her solicitor that Kevin did not intend to contest the divorce. Her solicitor had warned that he might contest her filing under the grounds of unreasonable behaviour, citing her alleged affair. Neither of them thought he would give her the divorce so easily. She was sceptical and wondered if Kevin was playing some sort of game. Would he change his mind? But her solicitor assured her that he was probably complying with the divorce to gain favour with the judge for his upcoming sentencing. But she warned Abi that the division of marital assets might not be so easily settled. Abi had found out that Mr McKendry was one of the best family solicitors in the London area. He had a track record of securing favourable outcomes for his clients. But she couldn't fault her own legal team. They didn't have fancy offices or flash cars, but they were hard-working and dedicated to getting Abi a good result.

Abi's days were full. When she wasn't looking after Emma, she was attending counselling and support groups and filling out forms and researching which benefits she was eligible for. Once the school holidays had begun, Emma had her cousins to play with during the day, which gave Abi more time to herself. Evelyn insisted that Abi join her at her weekly yoga classes and made sure she looked after herself. Whether it was a soak in the bath or reading a book in the garden, Evelyn made sure Abi had some down time.

Abi had heard from Glenda that Kevin's arrest had been the talk of the town. Although Glenda hadn't confirmed or denied the gossip, people had put two and two together and assumed that Kevin was to blame for Abi and Emma's disappearance. He became *persona non grata* and never showed his face at football or the pub again. He put their house up for sale, and it was rumoured that he had moved to a fancy apartment in London and had been dating a string of young women. Abi had mixed feelings about this. It was a huge relief that Kevin had moved away so she could return to Grovewood, but she was angry and resentful that he could just run away and continue with his life as if nothing had happened.

Abi hadn't seen Henry since the day he had brought her to Milton Keynes, but they'd kept in touch by phone. They texted each other sporadically through the day and, every night Abi counted down the minutes to his phone call. For the first few days, their conversations were slightly awkward. Neither knew what to say, so they kept things light and simply enjoyed the sound of the other's voice. But as the weeks progressed their conversations became more intimate, veering towards romantic. Henry was dying to see her but didn't want to impose, so he waited quietly for her to ask him.

He didn't have to wait too long.

On the sixth Saturday that Abi had been in Milton Keynes, she jumped out of bed like a child on Christmas morning. Today, Henry and Toby were coming for lunch. She ran around tidying the house and making sure everything was perfect, but soon gave up as the children took almost every toy that she put away straight back out. Evelyn refused her offer of help to prepare lunch and Javid insisted he could vacuum without her supervision. So, with nothing else to do, she went upstairs for a bubble bath.

After her bath, she went into the bedroom to get ready. Emma was standing at the window, waiting. "Why aren't they here yet?" She sounded sulky.

Abi checked the clock. It was still thirty minutes before they were due. "A few more minutes, honey." She selected a pair of crisp white cut-offs to go with the blue-and-white sleeveless tie-dye top she'd treated herself to for the occasion. After drying her hair, she reached for her straighteners, then had a better idea. She nipped into Evelyn's bedroom and borrowed her curling tongs instead. Then she applied some subtle make-up. She was just trying to decide if perfume would be too much when she heard Emma screech.

"They're here!" She bounded down the stairs and out of the front door. Abi wasn't too far behind. She got to the door just in time to see Emma throw her arms around Henry. She had to hold back her tears as she watched them hug. She hadn't realised how much she had missed him, and Emma was thrilled to see him too.

Henry made a funny face and pointed to the car. "Shall we get Toby out of the car, or shall we just leave him there?"

Emma giggled and looked at the back seat of the car, where Toby was frantically knocking on the window. "We can't leave him there!" she cried.

Henry ruffled her hair and handed her the car keys. He showed her which button to push and soon Toby was free. He jumped out of the car and followed Emma down the driveway and into the house. Henry returned to the car and retrieved a bouquet of flowers.

"Oh Henry, you shouldn't have." Abi held out her hand, but he pulled them away.

"Um, I didn't. These are for Evelyn. I couldn't turn up for lunch empty-handed."

"Of course not." She was trying to recover from her embarrassment when he produced a single red rose from behind the bouquet.

"This one is for you."

"Thank you." She brushed his hand lightly as she took the rose, then brought it to her nose and inhaled its sweet scent. "Come in."

Evelyn was waiting eagerly in the hall and greeted Henry with a huge smile. "Don't worry, Toby has already gone through to the garden. Emma is showing him off to her cousins. I can see why she likes him – he's adorable. He looks just like you."

Henry pretended not to notice Abi making a subtle 'shut up and get out of here' gesture to Evelyn, who took the hint and reached for the flowers. "I'll just pop these in some water for Abi."

"Actually, they're for you. A thank you for inviting us to lunch, and for the lovely dinner the last time I was here."

"You didn't have to, but thank you." She spied the single red rose in Abi's hand. "Why don't you two talk in the living room? I'll let you know when lunch is on the table." She disappeared quickly.

They went into the living room and Abi closed the door behind them. Henry was about to sit down on one of the two armchairs but at the last second diverted to the sofa instead. She sat close beside him and her perfume caught his nose. He recognised the scent; it was the one she'd worn the day at the park when they'd almost kissed.

He had been a bit apprehensive since she'd invited him to lunch. Their chats on the phone were amazing, but he was worried that he might have imagined the growing connection between them, but the familiar smell of Abi's perfume and the memory it evoked helped him relax. And by the way she was clutching the single red rose to her chest, he knew that they were finally in the same place. He reached for her hand and they interlaced their fingers. "I'm so happy to see you. You look amazing, by the way."

"Thank you."

"But how are you feeling? We haven't talked too much about the ins and outs of what's going on. You've sounded OK on the phone, but I get the impression that you're trying to put on a brave front for me. You don't need to do that. Please tell me how you have really been."

She shrugged. "Up and down. Inside out. Back to front. But I think I'm getting there. Finding a new normal, if that's possible."

"Everything's possible. And you're a testament to that. I'm so proud of the way you've handled everything."

"I couldn't have done it without everyone's help and support. My sister. Javid's family have been amazing. Glenda's been on the phone every other day. And I've made a good friend at a support group I've been going to. You wouldn't believe the terrible time she had before she got away from her husband."

Henry just nodded and tried to work out whether he was allowed to be upset that she hadn't mentioned him among the people who had been there for her. He would have stayed in Milton Keynes if she had let him.

He would have made the journey up and down every day if that's what she had wanted him to do. But he thought he'd done the right thing by giving her the space she had asked for. Had he made a huge mistake?

Suddenly her hand was on his knee. "Henry, I don't know what brought you to my house that night. But I do know that if you hadn't had been there, I wouldn't be where I am now. I can never repay you for all that you've done for me. You gave me a strength I didn't know I had. I'm so grateful to have you in my life." She squeezed his knee and looked up at him.

"I'd like to tell you why I was there that night. If you'll let me?"

She nodded.

"I'd been out on a date with Colette."

Abi pulled her hand from his knee. "Colette." She cleared her throat. "How are things going with you two?"

Henry tried to reassure her. "Don't worry, nothing happened. Well, something happened. I was out on a date with a pretty woman – we'd had a nice meal and the conversation was interesting enough. It should have been the perfect date, but all I could think about was you. Everything she did, I compared to you. Her hair was up; yours would have been down. She ordered red wine; you'd have had white. She had steak; you'd probably have chosen chicken. We talked about films; you and I would have talked about books. I cut the date short and I went to your house. I was going to tell you that I loved you. And I was going to beg you to leave your husband."

She shifted in her seat.

"I know you're going through an awful time right now, and I want to help in any way I can. Even if that means keeping my distance. I won't put you under any pressure. I'll wait for you as long as it takes – I just need to know that you want me to."

A smile spread over her face and she nodded, "I want you to."

He took her hands in his. "I see you in my future, Abigail. Emma too. And no matter what happens with Kevin, I promise I'll cherish that little girl. I'll treat her as if she was my own." A single tear ran down her cheek and he gently wiped it away.

"She'd like that. She's asked a few times if she and Toby could be brother and sister."

"I suppose they'll be as good as … if we ever get married."

She nudged him. "You're thinking about marriage already, and we've never even been out on a date?"

"Oh, I've definitely thought about it. Abigail Archer sounds really nice. But like I said, there's absolutely no pressure. We can take things slowly."

"Thank you. I think I'm getting close to being ready, but I don't know how much longer I can wait to find out how soft your lips are."

"You don't have to wait any more."

They moved in close to one another. Just as their lips were about to meet, Evelyn opened the door. "Lunch is ready!" She gasped when she saw them pull away from each other. "Oh my God! I'm *so* sorry. Just come in whenever you're ready." Smirking, she closed the door behind her.

They turned back to each other. Abi giggled and bit her lip. "That was a bit of a mood killer."

"Was it?" He leaned towards her and cupped his hand around the back of her neck. He slid his other hand around her waist to draw her tightly against him.

He'd imagined this moment so many times, but now their bodies were actually touching and her lips had never been as close. His heart was pounding as his lips met hers and he kissed her for the first time.

Her eyes drifted closed as his soft, tender kisses grew in intensity. A rush of adrenaline surged through her body when she discovered that his lips were incredibly soft and that his touch was both gentle and firm. She clung to him and kissed him back with all the passion and hunger that had been building inside her for months. It felt like there was nothing in that moment but them, together, and she wanted the moment to last forever.

Suddenly, Henry broke the embrace. The look she gave him showed her disappointment. He ran his hand through her hair and rested it on her cheek, caressing her gently. "What about lunch?"

She glanced at the closed door then back at him. "What about one more kiss?"

After lunch, Abi asked Henry to join her for a walk. Walks were now an important part of her daily routine: a chance for her to get away from all distractions and clear her head. But today she wanted to spend some more time alone with Henry. They had a lot to talk about.

The afternoon sun was burning in the sky, but a light breeze kept them cool as they walked hand in hand along the riverside path. During their phone calls Abi had tried to keep the conversation on normal, everyday things. Talking about Kevin at her counselling sessions was always upsetting and led to tears and she didn't want to worry Henry, especially when he was so far away.

He listened quietly as she explained what had happened and what was going to happen.

"I heard from my solicitor that Kevin is going to plead guilty to the assault. That means I won't have to testify in court, or even be in the same room as him. Instead, I'll give a victim impact statement, which the judge will take into account when deciding on Kevin's sentence. It's such a weight off my mind…"

"But?"

"My solicitor is urging me to pursue further abuse charges. She says I would have a very strong case against Kevin to charge him with coercive control. There have been some changes in the law relating to domestic abuse and it is getting easier to get a conviction."

"That sounds promising."

She shook her head. "Does it? It means there would be a trial, and I'm not sure I could cope with that. Kevin is going to plead guilty to domestic assault – he probably won't go to prison, but he'll receive a conviction. I think that's enough for me. I want this whole thing to be over with as quickly as possible. I want to move on with my life."

Henry frowned. "But that would mean Kevin would get away with the years of abuse he has inflicted on you – his wife, the woman he vowed to love and protect. And what if he does the same to another woman in the future?"

"My solicitor explained something called the 'right to ask'. It's also known as Clare's Law. If a future partner suspects that Kevin might have a history of domestic abuse, they can contact the police and ask them to look up Kevin, so they'll find out about his conviction. There's not much more I can do. Maybe I'm looking for the easiest way out. But I haven't decided yet. There's still time."

"Whatever you decide to do, I'll be right behind you. Anything you need, just let me know."

"Thank you." She squeezed his hand. "It's all so overwhelming. My other solicitor, the one handling the divorce, got a proposed settlement letter from Kevin's solicitor yesterday. Kevin has offered to pay a monthly sum for Emma's maintenance until she is eighteen, backdated to the day I left. He will also set up a trust fund in Emma's name which he will pay into monthly and she will get access to it when she turns twenty-one. He has also agreed to pay the full cost of my mum's nursing home for as long as she needs it."

Henry squinted. "That's very charitable."

"That's Kevin! He wants people to think he's charitable, but if you saw what he's offering me as a settlement, you might change your mind. My solicitor has advised me not to accept. She assures me that I have a very good case to get considerably more, but that might involve a long battle, and I'm tired. As long as he continues to support Emma and pay for Mum's care, I'll be OK. Money isn't important. And he's not fighting me for custody, but he does want to see Emma and she wants to see him. Under the circumstances, visits will take place at a contact centre and he will be supervised at all times. They'll be fortnightly visits at first, but they could become more frequent. Evie is going to take Emma to the sessions so that I don't have to be anywhere near Kevin and, if Evie isn't available, Emma's social worker will take her. I still can't get my head around the fact that my daughter needs a social worker. Emma has only seen Kevin once so far."

"How did it go?"

Abi grimaced. "Awful. She was so excited, she

asked me to go with her and sulked when I wouldn't. Evie said she was a complete pain in the car on the way there. Then she caused a scene when it was time to leave. Evie said Kevin played the distraught father routine. I don't know – maybe he does miss her, but he never paid her that much attention when we all lived together. I used to think he was a good father because he provided for his family. But when I see how you are with Toby, Javid with my nieces and nephew, and Glenda's husband with their kids, I realise he wasn't a good father at all. When I look back at it, all he did was shower her with gifts, or help her with her homework the odd time. And I can't help thinking that he didn't do those things for Emma; he did them to spite me."

They had been walking for about half an hour when Henry pointed to a bench by the river. They sat and took in the sun as they watched a family of swans feeding.

Henry smiled at Abi. "My head is spinning after all that. You've had so much on your plate, have you had time to think about where you and Emma are going to live? I suppose it would be nice to stay up here so you can be close to your sister."

She shook her head. "Kevin's selling the house and has moved back to London, so there's no reason we can't move back to Grovewood. I know it'll be hard – I'm sure I'm the talk of the town."

"No. People are on your side. You'll have plenty of support."

"I don't want people fussing. I just want to get back to normal. I've contacted the council and we're on the housing list. There are only a few people ahead of me, but they said it could be a few months before a house becomes available. I hope to get a part-time job. I was thinking that, now I'm going to be getting regular payments from Kevin, I might be able to rent privately. I've had a look at a few properties online, but they're all bigger houses, three or four bedrooms. I can't afford that. I'll keep looking, but it's frustrating. I really wanted to get back in time for September. I want Emma to start the school year with her friends."

"Um, I might know of somewhere you could live."

She narrowed her eyes at him. "Thank you, Henry. But we really can't stay with you. We need our own space."

"I know you can't stay with me. But how would you feel about staying near me?"

"Near you?"

"Yeah. One flat across and two storeys up, to be precise."

She squinted at him.

"I just found out that a flat in my building will be available at the end of August. You'll be cutting it fine for school, but it could work. I'll be close in case you ever have any trouble with Kevin. I can also help you with babysitting and school runs, especially if you're considering getting a job – save you spending all your money on childcare. I hope you don't mind, but I spoke to my landlord and explained your situation. He says you can have first refusal. But..."

"I knew there had to be a catch. It sounds too good to be true."

"There's a £500 security deposit and he needs the first month's rent up front. Also, it's not furnished. But I have a little money saved. I can help you if you need it."

"That is so sweet. But it's OK. I should have enough."

"So, you're OK with the idea? I'll be close but I'll

give you all the space and all the time you need. Everything will be on your terms."

"It sounds perfect, Henry. Thank you." Abi leaned towards him and kissed him softly on the lips, then giggled as she pulled away and looked at her watch. "I feel like a teenager with a curfew. We'd best get back. They'll be wondering where we are."

***

Abi spent the next few weeks planning and organising. She made a few trips back to Grovewood to see her mum and Henry, to view the new flat and look for work. She was offered a job in the same supermarket she and Glenda had worked in when they'd left school. Much to her delight, Saul was no longer the manager. The position belonged to a woman who had two children in secondary school. She was completely understanding of Abi's circumstances and offered her four shifts a week during school hours. It was perfect. Although Abi was daunted about going back to work after more than six years, she was excited at the prospect of regaining her independence – and hopefully her confidence along with it.

She trawled local buying and selling websites for second-hand furniture and other essentials for her new flat. She asked Henry to collect a few things, and he arranged to store them in his parents' garage until the flat was vacant.

The landlord had expected to have at least a week in between tenants to repaint the flat and do some minor repairs, but in the end, he only had two days. Emma was due to start school and Abi was eager to start her new job. But the main reason Abi wanted to move in soon was that she was desperate for her own space. Although she loved her sister and her family dearly, it was so noisy there; she was used to a quieter life. Henry and the landlord came to an agreement. The landlord would do the minor repairs and pay for the paint and Henry would do the painting. But when Henry got the keys to the flat, he soon realised the enormity of the task. He decided that, in the short time available, he could either do lots of small jobs or concentrate on one big job. He remembered Abi mentioning on the phone that she was disappointed not to have Emma's bedroom ready for their arrival, as she thought it might help her settle in. She had described what she wanted it to look like, so Henry decided the small jobs could be done over time, and he'd focus on making Emma's room perfect.

***

Henry was doing a last-minute tidy-up in the flat when Abi rang to say she had arrived. He rushed to the door of the flat and buzzed them up, then stood out in the hall and waited. Soon the lift doors opened and Abi and Emma stepped out. He beamed at them and held his arms out to Emma. "Welcome home."

Emma was unusually quiet. She didn't give him her usual hug but clung to her doll and tried to hide behind Abi's leg.

"Is everything OK?" Henry asked.

Abi shrugged and rolled her eyes.

Henry knelt down to Emma and made a funny face. "There's someone in the kitchen waiting for you with juice and cookies."

She gave a small smile and went to join Toby in

the kitchen.

"What's up with her?"

"She saw Kevin again yesterday. God knows what he said to her. He gave her that doll, among other things, and she's clung to it ever since. When we were leaving Evie's, she said that she'd changed her mind. She didn't want to live in a flat after all, and if she couldn't stay at her cousins' house, why couldn't she just go home? I told her the flat would be really cosy and we'd be so close to Toby she could see him all the time, but she sulked the whole way down in the car. I must have driven that journey a hundred times over the years, but it's never felt so long."

"Well, you're here now. Come on in and we'll give the kettle a test drive." He stood back and let her walk into her new flat.

She gave him a sad smile and walked in. She'd expected to find all her new furniture in a pile in the living room, but Henry had laid everything out. There was even a vase of flowers on the nest of tables, and a colourful rug on the floor. "Henry, you said you hadn't done much. This is amazing."

"I just threw a few cushions down. But I can come over at weekends. Between the two of us, we'll get this place shipshape and Bristol fashion in no time."

"Thank you." This time her smile was genuine.

He showed her into the kitchen, where the kids sat at a small dining table. Toby was trying to show Emma his new Transformer but she wasn't interested. She just stared at her doll. The worry on Abi's face made Henry's heart sink. This wasn't how it was supposed to go. He wanted so much for this to be a happy moment for them to remember. It was time to unveil the surprise.

"Abigail, why don't you take Emma down to her new bedroom?" He winked at her and she gave him a confused look.

"OK. Come on, sweetheart. Let's show your dolly where she can sleep."

Reluctantly Emma got up from her chair and followed her mum down the hall. Henry and Toby followed. They stopped at a door on which *Emma* was painted in pink calligraphy.

Abi touched Henry's arm. "That's really sweet."

Emma pushed the door open then let out a loud gasp. "A unicorn!" She ran into the room, grabbed the giant stuffed unicorn and held it close. Toby squeezed in past Henry and joined her beside a pile of stuffed toys. He selected his favourite and the two began to play.

Abi's eyes were wide as she looked around the room. Fairy lights were strung like bunting across the walls, which were pastel pink, apart from the wall behind the bed, which was pale grey. The bed itself was a pink carriage with a tulle canopy that hung from the ceiling. The *Frozen* duvet cover was strewn with fluffy pink and purple cushions. There was a white wardrobe, a small bookshelf full of books and a small desk and chair. On top of the desk were colouring pencils and a huge colouring pad.

Henry held his breath as he turned to Abi, who hadn't said a word. He was worried that he'd done it wrong. Tears were streaming down her cheeks. "Is it OK?"

"Oh, Henry!" She threw her arms around him and hugged him tightly. "Thank you so much. It's perfect."

"I'm glad you like it. Unfortunately, your bedroom isn't as perfect. We'll do that one next."

"I've been sharing a single bed with Emma for

over two months. As long as I get to sleep without little knees and elbows in my back, I'll be happy."

"Give me your keys. I'll go down to the car and start bringing up your stuff."

"Thanks. I just brought the essentials. Evie is going to bring another car-load down next weekend."

"Great. Why don't you make us a cup of tea? Oh, and I've left you a little housewarming gift on the kitchen counter."

She remembered the expensive clock she was going to buy as a housewarming gift for him. He'd better not have, she thought. "Henry?"

He tapped his finger against the side of his nose and hurried off down to the car.

Henry didn't want to outstay his welcome on their first night, so after a cup of tea and a few cookies, he made his apologies. "I hope you don't mind, but I have to get Toby over to Becca's. I'll let you two settle into your new home. If you need anything, give me a shout."

"Thanks. And thank you again for the present." She pointed to the bundle of tea towels on the worktop. "The perfect housewarming gift."

"I knew you'd like it. Good luck for tomorrow, girls. Perhaps you could give me a quick phone call tomorrow night, just to let me know how your first days went?" He stood up and beckoned Toby to do the same.

"Of course. I'm sure we'll have plenty to tell you." She walked them to the door. Henry wasn't sure whether to kiss her in front of Toby or not, so he leaned in, gave her a quick peck on the cheek then hurried out of the door. "Good night."

"Night, Henry. Night, Toby." She closed the door behind them and took a deep breath. She walked around the flat, trying to let everything sink in. She thought she'd be more apprehensive, but she already felt comfortable there. But she wasn't sure if that was just because she knew Henry was so close.

Chapter Nineteen

For the next few weeks, Henry gave Abi lots of space. He didn't call over without an invitation, and he asked Abi and Emma down to his flat for dinner with him and Toby. He did insist that they resume their standing date at soft play each Saturday but, instead of meeting there, they met in the car park of their building and took turns driving. Then at the end of September, when he was sure that Abi had adjusted to working life and Emma had settled back into school, Henry asked Abi out on a proper date.

Abi glanced at her watch as she hurried into the living room. She was wearing a little black dress and matching stiletto heels. She struck a pose in front of Glenda and Emma, who were sprawled on the sofa. "What do you think?"

Emma, who barely took her eyes off the television, gave her mum a thumbs-up. Glenda attempted a wolf whistle. "Beautiful. But you also looked beautiful in the last three dresses. I don't know why you're so nervous. Henry likes you for who you are, not what you're wearing."

"I know, but it's our first real date. I want everything to be perfect."

"Oh, now I get it." Glenda smirked and gestured to Emma. "Are you sure you don't want us to go to my house?"

"I didn't mean *that*!" Abi fanned her face. *Well, not tonight anyway...*

"I'll have Emma in bed nice and early. Just in case."

"Stop it! So, the dress – yes?"

"Are you comfortable?"

"Not in these heels."

"Then change them."

There was a knock at the door.

"Quickly. I'll get the door." Glenda hurried to the front door and opened it to find Henry shifting from foot to foot.

"Evening, Glenda," he said with a smile.

She scanned him up and down. He was wearing a black suit with a crisp off-white open-collared shirt. She smiled when she saw the two red roses in his hand. "Hi, Henry."

He blushed.

"You look well. Come in." She stepped back and let him walk in past her, then followed him to the living room.

He went straight to the sofa and knelt down in front of Emma. He offered her one of the roses. "Hi sweetie. This is for you." She didn't reply, but took the rose and set it on the sofa beside her. He turned to Glenda. "Is everything OK?"

Glenda mouthed, "Kevin!"

Henry groaned as he got up, then noticed Abi at the door. She had been watching them and had seen how dismissive Emma had been of Henry. Her heart went out to them both. Emma was still coming to terms with her new life. Although she was fond of Henry, she desperately missed her daddy. Henry knew he could never replace Kevin, but was slowly figuring out how to cultivate his new relationship with Emma. Abi gave Henry a sympathetic smile. He beamed back at her, then approached and offered her the rose. "Good evening, Abigail. May I say you look beautiful."

"You may." She curtseyed and took the flower. They gazed into each other's eyes for a few seconds until they were interrupted by Henry's phone, which beeped in his pocket.

"That'll be the taxi."

Abi grabbed her shawl from the armchair and wrapped it around her bare shoulders. She stopped at the sofa and kissed Emma on the top of her head. "Enjoy your movie. There are some treats on the kitchen counter, and don't forget to brush your teeth. Night, night."

"Have a good time, you two." Glenda winked.

"Night, Mummy."

Abi narrowed her eyes at Emma and gestured to Henry.

"Night, Henry," Emma whispered.

"Night, sweetie." Henry ruffled her hair, which coaxed a small smile from her. Then he turned to Abi and held out his hand. "Shall we?"

Abi had a quick glance at the menu and then set it down on the table. She wasn't overly hungry, which was a good thing, because the butterflies in her stomach would probably ruin her meal anyway. She looked over at Henry, who was still studying the menu, then around at the other people in the restaurant. This was the first time she'd been out in public with Henry when she wasn't concerned about who saw them, but she was aware that people might still be talking about what had happened with Kevin. She raised her hand to the scar on her temple, but at the last second scratched her nose instead. Her therapist had been the one to point out her subconscious reflex when she thought about Kevin. But this was not a time to reflect on the past, but to enjoy the present. She took a deep breath and looked at Henry.

"See anything you like?"

He set the menu down and stared into her eyes. "Yes. But not on the menu. You, look incredible tonight."

"Thank you. You look great too. Although, before I forget, would you mind taking the kids to soft play by yourself next Saturday? I've been offered an extra shift at work."

"No problem. I'll bring a book, so I don't miss you too much." He winked. "You seem to really like working at the supermarket."

"I love it. Everyone's really nice, and there's this little old lady who comes in — she remembers me from last time I worked there. She looks at me like a long-lost friend. And it won't be every Saturday — I don't want to miss out on precious time with you and the kids — but it's the first time they've asked me and I don't want to turn them down in case they don't ask again. I could really do with the extra money; I need to start thinking about Christmas. I'm certain Kevin's still planning that bloody pony to upstage me. The idiot probably thinks he can keep it in his penthouse." She noticed Henry had shifted in his seat. "I'm sorry. But he makes me so cross. I got word from my solicitor that he's got his hearing next week. He'll likely get a suspended sentence."

Henry's jaw tightened.

"But then it will be over, and we're close to finalising the divorce as well. It will be official in the next week or two. Although I want to reassess the visitation arrangements. Kevin missed another one this afternoon."

"Not again! So that's why Emma was so down."

"Yep. He didn't even phone to let us know this time. I presume he was out last night and was too hungover. It's so unfair on Emma – she was devastated and sulked in her room most of the day. Even when he does show up, she misbehaves for a few days afterwards. Her counsellor says she's just acting out and it will pass, so I can just about bear it when she takes her anger and frustration out on me, but I feel terrible when she gives you the cold shoulder."

"She was a bit frosty this evening, but I understand that. She's just a child, she doesn't mean it. She'll be fine with me in a day or two."

Abi sighed. She was so grateful for Henry. He was rational, compassionate and so very patient – the complete opposite of Kevin. Why on earth had she ever thought that Kevin was a good father? She was also struggling to remember why she fell in love with him. Her therapist had explained that he may well have shown signs of abusive behaviour at the beginning of the relationship, but that Kevin was good at seduction, he knew what she wanted, and he had been able to sell her the perfect marriage. He had waited until she was in love with him before he began to criticise her, belittle her and strip her of her confidence, so he had full control over her. He brainwashed her into thinking that *she* was the problem in the relationship. But she now knew that that had never been the case. Sadly, it had taken the assault to open her eyes to who he truly was. Even at that point, if she hadn't had the support of Henry, Evelyn and Glenda, Kevin might have been able to make her think that it had been her fault too. And how long would it have been until he hit her again? She struggled not to cry at the thought and took a deep breath instead. She was rediscovering herself through therapy, self-care and exercise, and she wasn't going to let Kevin rule – or ruin – her life any further.

She tapped her index finger on the table. "This can't continue. I let Kevin treat me like crap for years, but I'll be damned if I'm going to let him do the same to my daughter. I'm going to phone my solicitor first thing on Monday morning. If Kevin really wants to see Emma, he's going to have to prove it, because I'm not going to make it easy for him." She nodded, a determined look in her eyes.

Henry was taken aback. "Remind me never to get on the wrong side of you, Abigail Preston."

"And that won't be my name for much longer either. Once I'm divorced, I'm going to change back to my maiden name."

"Which is?"

"McIntyre."

"It suits you."

"It should, because it's my real name." She stuck her tongue out at him. "But let's not talk about Kevin any more. This is our first date. You've had one of these more recently than I have. What do people talk about on a first date these days?"

"They ask questions and talk about the things that we already know about each other. This date is just a formality, Abigail. Albeit a rather pleasant one. I'm already head over heels in love with you."

She bit her lip. "That makes two of us."

"Then why change your name? Seems like a lot of hassle, especially if you ever want to get married again."

That wasn't the first time he'd mentioned marriage – and she'd imagined it countless times. But she was enjoying her new independence and was working through her emotional issues with her therapist. She knew she wanted to be with Henry, but she wasn't going to let him be complacent about it. "Oh, behave! Let me get rid of one husband before I saddle myself with another one."

"Hey!" He pretended to be offended.

"You're not even divorced yet. So there's no rush. Is there?"

He reached across the table for her hand. "Of course not. And I stand by my promise not to pressure you. I just want to make sure that you're open to the possibility of getting married again. One day."

She'd imagined much more than just marrying Henry. Since he'd told her that he hoped to have another child, she had wondered what their baby might look like, and how Emma would react to having a new brother or sister. She'd also imagined a lovely little house that they would all live in. She hated living in her flat. Emma did too. They had only been there for six weeks and they already yearned for some outside space. But she tried her best not to lament over what she used to have and to be grateful for what she had, and what she would have in the future.

Henry cleared his throat. "I hope that daydream you're having features a house with a garden. Outside space is a must for me. And I'm thinking at least three bedrooms, for the nights we have Toby. Although maybe we should get one with four. Just in case we—" He stopped and looked over at Abi. She gave him a loving smile.

"All in good time, Henry." She picked up her wine glass and took a sip. "Let's start with dinner."

Epilogue

Over the next few months, Abi and Henry spent most of their free time together and he gradually, and unofficially, moved into Abi's flat. He only stayed in his own flat on the nights he had Toby. The children loved having each other as company for activities, days out and just lounging round on rainy afternoons.

The supervised visits between Emma and Kevin stopped, at Abi's insistence. As she had expected, Kevin did not put up much of a fight. His parents, on the other hand, contacted Abi through her solicitor and asked if they could see Emma. After careful consideration and speaking to them and Emma, Abi agreed, but everything was to be on her terms. They were very gracious. Although they never mentioned the assault, the hug that Kevin's mother gave Abi, along with the look of sympathy in her eyes, said more than words ever could. Emma loved the fuss and attention her grandparents lavished on her, and after a few visits begged Abi to let her spend a weekend with them. Abi knew that Emma would be happy and safe in their care, so agreed to let Emma spend one weekend a month with them for as long as Emma was happy with the arrangement.

Abi also agreed to let Kevin visit Emma while she was at his parents' house – on the condition that he was never there when she dropped off Emma or picked her up. Abi also insisted that Kevin's mother was to be in charge at all times and Kevin was to be completely sober.

Henry made a special effort to spend time with Emma. He learned how to put her hair in plaits, helped her with her homework and read her bedtime stories. In return, she taught him the names of her dolls and the words to all of the songs from *Frozen*. Abi was delighted at the special bond that was forming between them. She was forming her own bond with Toby, especially since she had begun to pick him up from school and look after him every day.

One afternoon, Henry turned his key in the door of Abi's flat and hurried inside. "Abigail?"

"In the kitchen."

Henry rushed into the kitchen and found her at the table, surrounded by paperwork. "Where are the kids?" he asked, out of breath.

"Emma's playing in her room and Becca's already picked Toby up. Why?"

"Because when I got your text telling me to get up here, I thought there was something wrong."

"I'm so sorry. I didn't mean to worry you. I have something exciting to tell you." She looked up at him and pursed her lips. He kissed her, then he pulled out a chair and sat beside her at the table.

"I had a missed call on my phone when I was driving home from school. It was the jeweller. He's found a buyer for the last of my jewellery. It's nowhere near what it cost new, but if we add that to what we've already saved, it'll really help out with the deposit."

"Great!" He reached over to hug her, but she pushed him away.

"There's more. I updated our budget with the £11,000 I just got for my jewellery. Even if we don't count the pay increment you're due, we can now comfortably afford the deposit and the repayments for…" She chose a property brochure from the pile on the table and held it up for him to see. It was a four-bedroom house that had everything they wanted. But they hadn't been to view it as it had been out of their price range – until now.

"I thought that was just wishful thinking."

"Well, it looks like you might just get what you wished for."

He squeezed her knee. "I've already got it." He gave her a long kiss, then took the brochure and examined it. "You're so good at all this stuff. You should be managing that supermarket. So, when are we going to go and see it?"

"I'll be on the phone at 9 a.m. tomorrow to arrange a viewing."

"I can't wait. And we should celebrate. I know it's my night to cook, but do you think the budget could stretch to some fish and chips?"

Abi nodded.

"Should I get a bottle of wine? We can snuggle on the sofa with a soppy movie once Emma's in bed."

"That sounds perfect. But there's a chance you'll have to drink the wine by yourself. I bought this today." She slid something out from under the pile of papers on the table. He squinted at it.

"Is that a pregnancy test?" His mouth fell open. *"Already?"*

She smirked. "I haven't taken it yet; I was waiting for you. But I've felt a bit off the past few days. And I'm late. I'm never late."

"Oh my God!" He lifted her up and spun her around. As soon as he set her back on her feet, he grabbed the test from the table and held his hand out to her. "Let's go and take it now."

"What about Emma?"

"She'll be OK in her room. And if she does come in, she can wait with us. Come on."

She took his hand and they hurried to the bathroom. Abi stopped at the door. "Wait here. I'll call you in."

"Good luck." He blew her a kiss as she closed the door.

They held hands and perched on the edge of the bath to wait. The two minutes felt like forever. Abi looked over at Henry, who had a smile on his face and his eyes closed. She closed her eyes too and her mind drifted back to when she found out she was pregnant with Emma. Her period was late, so she called Kevin's mobile to tell him she was thinking of taking a test. He didn't answer or call her back, so she waited until he got home from work, surprised him with the unwrapped test and suggested they do it together. He said there was a football match on TV that he wanted to watch and told her just to let him know. She had been so excited to find out, but spending those two minutes alone in the bathroom took the shine off the good news. Kevin had barely cracked a smile when she told him; maybe she should have known then what lay ahead. She looked over at Henry then down at her phone. One more minute.

Henry kept his eyes shut. He'd been in this position before, perched on the side of the bath with Becca. He loved kids and wanted a family, but he and Becca had only been dating for three months and he didn't think they were ready. He hoped the test would be negative. When the two minutes were up and they saw it was positive, Becca began to cry. Henry thought at first they were tears of joy, but when he saw the look on her face, he realised that she was terrified. He was too. They had never even talked about having a baby. At the time it felt like the worst moment in his life, but once the news sank in and they'd talked it over, he was excited and threw himself into making preparations for the baby. He was over the moon when Toby was born and took to being a father like a duck to water. He desperately wanted another child but Becca wasn't keen.

He glanced over at Abi. This time it was completely different: he was desperate for the test to be positive, and he knew Abi's tears would be of joy because they had talked about trying for a baby. Abi had stopped taking the pill, but they had assumed it would take a few months for her fertility to return. They never imagined it would happen so quickly.

The alarm sounded on Abi's phone. The two minutes were up. She kept her eyes closed and held the test out to Henry. "I can't look. Just tell me. Yes or no."

He looked down at the test and an enormous grin spread over his face. He nudged Abi. "We're definitely going to need that fourth bedroom."

She stared, wide-eyed, at the two blue lines. She couldn't stop tears from streaming down her cheeks.

"Please tell me they're happy tears," he said.

"They're happy tears. Are you happy?"

"Not just happy. I'm ecstatic! And the kids will be too. Just wait until they find out they're getting a baby brother or sister."

"I know, but they're six already. Are we crazy starting all over again?"

"Totally crazy. But I can't wait to start all over

again – with you." Then he frowned. "This is perfect but, if I'm honest, I *could* be happier." He went down on one knee and pretended to take something out of his pocket. He held up an imaginary box and pretended to open it. "Abigail, will you marry me?"

"I'm so glad there's no ring in that fake box." She held her hands out to him and helped him up. "What are you doing? I thought I had already said yes. When we decided to try for a baby, we said we'd get married someday. I told you, I don't need a ring."

"But it's not official until there's a ring."

"Believe me, it's official. We will get married and when we do, all I want is a simple gold band."

"But you're divorced, I will be soon, and things have changed. We can't have a baby out of wedlock. It wouldn't be appropriate, would it?"

She stuck her tongue out at him. "Good! I'm done with being appropriate. I don't care if we live in sin forever." She put her arms around his neck and rubbed her nose against his. "In our house. With my child, your child, and our child."

"You're right. That's all that matters – that we're together as a proper family. And it might be in that house you found. It looks perfect. It's everything we want. Even the..." He trailed off.

"The what?"

"Nothing. It's silly. It's just... Well, the brochure says the house has floored roof space. And I was thinking that—"

"We could turn it into your library?"

"How did you know?"

"Because I was thinking the same thing. We could get you a small sofa or daybed, and maybe set up a children's corner with some beanbags or tiny chairs. All your books will be on display. It'll be perfect."

He wrapped his arms around her. "It will be perfect. There's even going to be a special space reserved for your Kindle. It's going to be *our* library."

Acknowledgements

Well, I've written another book. Who knew it would take longer than the first one? Along the way, I've made some new friends, reconnected with old ones, and even gathered a small group of fans.

Special thanks to all my family and friends for supporting me throughout the process, and for your help in promoting my books.

Thank you to returning beta readers: Jen, Mags, Lynda and Helen. I hope you will all be on board for book three ☺.

Thanks to my editor, Jane H. Your notes really made a difference.

Big thanks to Aaron & Jane for the wonderful cover.

Thank you to my friends on Twitter for your help and encouragement.

And last but not least, thank you to my readers! I hope you enjoyed Waiting for Saturday, and I'll try and get another book out soon. In the meantime, I'd be grateful if you could find the time to leave a review on Amazon or Goodreads, or even just word of mouth to a friend.

As always, feel free to pop by and say hello on your preferred social media channel.

About the Author

Catherine Morrison lives in Lisburn, Northern Ireland with her husband and two children. When she's not at her paid job or spending time with her family, she is writing or thinking about writing. So please don't ask her about the latest mini-series because she doesn't have time to watch TV.

Waiting for Saturday is Catherine's second novel. Originally intended for release in 2020, it was delayed by – well, you know – but don't worry, it's not mentioned in the book.

Catherine is currently working on the much-anticipated sequel to her first novel, The Hook, as well as a gritty second chance romance. Keep an eye on her social media for details.

catherinemorrisonauthor

wouldbewriter

@would_bewriter

Printed in Great Britain
by Amazon

58574760R00129